A CANADIAN HEROINE

HEROINE

A Novel

Volume 1

Mrs. Harry Coghill

1ST WORLD
LIBRARY
Literary Society

A Canadian Heroine, Volume 1

Mrs. Harry Coghill

© 1st World Library – Literary Society, 2006
PO Box 2211
Fairfield, IA 52556
www.1stworldlibrary.org
First Edition

LCCN: 2006930771

Softcover ISBN: 1-4218-2182-6
Hardcover ISBN: 1-4218-2082-X
eBook ISBN: 1-4218-2282-2

Purchase *"A Canadian Heroine, Volume 1"*
as a traditional bound book at:
www.1stWorldLibrary.org/purchase.asp?ISBN=1-4218-2182-6

1st World Library Literary Society is a nonprofit
organization dedicated to promoting literacy by:

- Creating a free internet library accessible from any
computer worldwide.
- Hosting writing competitions and offering book
publishing scholarships.

Readers interested in supporting literacy
through sponsorship, donations or
membership please contact:
literacy@1stworldlibrary.org
Check us out at: www.1stworldlibrary.ORG
and start downloading free ebooks today.

A Canadian Heroine, Volume 1
contributed by Tim, Ed & Rodney
in support of
1st World Library Literary Society

"Questa chiese Lucia in suo dimando,
E disse: Or ha bisogno il tuo fedele
Di te, e io a te lo raccomando."

- Inferno. Canto II.

"Qu'elles sont belles, nos campagnes;
En Canada qu'on vit content!
Salut o sublimes montagnes,
Bords du superbe St. Laurent!
Habitant de cette contree
Que nature veut embellir,
Tu peux marcher tete levee,
Ton pays doit t'enorgueillir."

-J. Bedard.

CHAPTER I

It was near sunset, and the season was early summer. Every tree was in full leaf, but the foliage had still the exquisite freshness of its first tints, undimmed by dust or scorching heat. The grass was, for the present, as green as English grass, but the sky overhead was more glorious than any that ever bent above an English landscape. So far away it rose overhead, where colour faded into infinite space, that the eye seemed to look up and up, towards the Gate of Heaven, and only through mortal weakness to fail in reaching it. Low down around the horizon there was no blue, but pure, pale green depths, where clouds floated, magnificent in deep rosy and golden splendour. Under such skies the roughest landscape, the wildest forest, softens into beauty; such light and colour, like fairy robes, glorify the most commonplace; but here, earth lent her own charms to be decked by heaven.

Through a quiet landscape went the river - the grand silent flood which by-and-by, many miles further on its course, would make Niagara. Here it flowed calmly, reflecting the sunset, a giant with its energies untaxed and its passions unroused - a kindly St. Christopher, yet capable of being transformed into a destroying Thor. Far away, seen over a low projecting point of land, white sails gleamed now and then, as ships moved upon the lake from whence the river came; and nearer, upon the great stream itself, a few boats were idling. In the bend formed by the point, and quite near the lake, lay a small town, its wooden wharves and warehouses lining the shore for some distance. Lower down, the bank rose high, dropping precipitously to the water's edge; and nearer still, the precipice changed to a steep, but green and wooded bank, and here, on the summit of the bank, stood Mrs. Costello's cottage.

It was a charming white nest, with a broad verandah all embowered in green, so placed as to look out upon the river through a screen of boughs and flowers. If you had seen Mrs. Costello and her daughter sitting upon the verandah, as they were tolerably sure to be found every day while summer lasted, you would have owned that it would be hard to find a prettier picture set in a prettier frame.

This evening they were there alone. Mrs. Costello had her work-table placed at the end nearest the river, and her rocking-chair beside it. Some knitting was in her hands, but she could not knit, for her ball of wool was being idly wound and unwound round her daughter's fingers.

Sitting on a footstool, leaning back against her mother's knee, was this daughter - a child loved (it could almost be seen at a glance) with an absorbing, passionate love. A girl of seventeen, just between child and woman, who seemed to have been a baby but yesterday, and who still, in the midst of her new womanly grace, kept her caressing baby ways. Something unusual, not only in degree but in kind, belonged to her brilliant beauty, and set it off. The marvellous blackness of hair and eyes was so soft in its depth, the tint of her skin so transparent in its duskiness, her slight figure so flexible, so exquisite in its outlines, that it was impossible not to wonder what the type was which produced so perfect an example. Spanish it was said to be, but the child was Canadian by birth, and her mother English; it was clear that whatever race had bestowed Lucia's dower of beauty, it had come to her through her father.

Mother and daughter often sat as now, silent and idle both; Lucia dreaming after her girlish fashion, and Mrs. Costello content to wait and let her life be absorbed in her child's. But to-night Lucia was dreaming of England, the far-away "home" which she had never seen, but of which almost all her elder friends spoke, and where her mother's childhood and girlhood had been passed. She still leaned her head back lazily as she began to talk.

"Are English sunsets as lovely as ours, Mamma?"

Mrs. Costello smiled. "I can't tell," she said; "they are as lovely to me, - but I only see them in memory."

"You have often talked about going home, when shall it be?"

"I have talked of *your* going, not of mine - *that* will never be."

"Mamma!" Lucia raised her head. She looked at her mother inquiringly, but somehow she felt that Mrs. Costello could not talk to her just then. A troubled expression crossed her own face for a moment, then she put down the ball of wool and laid her arms caressingly round her mother's waist.

But both again remained silent for many minutes, so silent that the faint wash of the river against the bank sounded plainly, and a woodpecker could be heard making his last tap-tap on a tree by the garden-gate.

By-and-by Mrs. Costello spoke again, as if there had been no interruption. "But about this picnic, Lucia; do you think it would be a great sacrifice to give it up?"

"A great sacrifice? Why, mamma, you must think me a baby to ask such a question. I stayed away from the best one last summer without breaking my heart."

"Last summer I thought you too young for large parties, but this year I have let you go - and, indeed, I do not forbid your going this time. Understand that clearly, my child. I have only fancy, not reason, to set against your wishes."

"Mother, you are not fanciful. Since you wish me to stay at

home, I wish it also. Forget the picnic altogether."

She sprang up, kissed her mother's forehead, and darted away to the further end of the verandah, bursting out into a gay song as she leaned over to gather a spray of pale prairie roses that climbed up the trellis-work. The pretty scentless blossoms were but just caught, when a rattling of wheels was heard on the stony lane which led from the high-road to the cottage.

"Who can be coming now? Margery is out, mamma, and the gate is fastened; I must go and open it."

She darted into the house on her errand - for the principal entrance was in the gable end of the building - but before she had had time to cross the parlour and hall to the outer door, the little garden-gate opened, and a very pretty woman in a grey cloak and straw hat came through, and up the verandah steps with the air of a person perfectly at home.

Mrs. Costello rose to meet her with an exclamation.

"Mrs. Bellairs! We never thought of it being you. Lucia is gone to open the gate."

"I found the little one open; so I left Bella to take care of Bob, and came round. In fact, I ought not to be here at all, but as I wanted to persuade you about to-morrow, I ran away the moment dinner was over, and must run back again instantly."

"Sit down, at any rate, while you *are* here."

She sat down, and taking off her hat, threw it on the floor.

"How delicious this is! I believe you don't know what heat means. I have been half dead all day, and not a moment's rest, I assure you, with the people continually coming to ask some stupid question or to borrow something. The house is half stripped now and I fully expect that before to-morrow night it will be emptied of everything movable in it."

"You are surely getting up something more elaborate than usual; do you expect to have so much pleasure?"

"Oh, I suppose the young people do. Of course, staid matrons like you and me," with a gay laugh, "cannot be quite so sanguine; but, however, they do expect great fun, and I came to *implore* you to let Lucia come. I assure you I won't answer for the consequences if she does not."

"Lucia shall go if she wishes it." Mrs. Costello spoke gravely, and stopped abruptly. She resumed, "You know I never leave home; and it may be excused to a mother who sees nothing of the world, to fear it a little for her only child."

"*Such* a child, too! She is growing perfectly lovely. But, then, dear Mrs. Costello, the very idea of calling our tiny backwood's society, 'the world;' and as for Lucia, if you *will* not come with her, I promise, at any rate, to take the same care of her as I will of my Flo when she is big enough to face our great world."

She spoke laughing, but with some earnestness under the sparkle of her bright eyes; and immediately afterwards rose, saying, "I suppose Bella cannot leave Bob, and Lucia will not leave Bella, so I must go to them; and if Lucia pleases, she may come to-morrow?"

"Yes, yes; I am foolish. She shall come, I promise you for her. And, indeed, I ought to thank you also."

"No, no; I can't expect to be thanked for committing a theft. Good-bye. I shall send Bella to fetch her. Good-bye."

She took up her hat, gave her friend a kiss, and ran down the steps and out again, through the wicket by which she had entered. A minute after the sound of her little carriage rolling away was heard, and Lucia came back flushed and puzzled.

"But, mamma, you have been overpersuaded. Indeed; I do not

want to go."

"I think you do, darling; or will do by-and-by. I have quite changed my mind, and promised Mrs. Bellairs to send you to her in the morning; so now all you have to do is to see that your things are ready. Two toilettes to prepare! What an event for such a country girl as you! Come in and let us see."

"Mamma, you know my things are all ready. I don't want to go in. I don't want to go."

"Lucia! Are *you* changeable, also, then?"

"No, mamma. At least not without cause."

Mrs. Costello smiled, "What is the cause at present?"

Lucia moved impatiently. "Oh, it is so stupid!" she said.

"What is stupid? A picnic?"

"No, people," and she laughed half shyly, half saucily, and blushed deeper still.

"What people?"

"Bella has been telling me - ;"

"Telling you what, my child? That people are stupid?"

Lucia sat down again in her old place, and pulled her mother back into hers. Then with her two elbows resting on Mrs. Costello's lap, and her red cheek hidden by her hands, she answered, with a comical sort of disdain and half-affected anger,

"Mamma, just think. At Mrs. Bellairs' to-day, at dinner, Mr. Percy was asking questions about what was going to be done to-morrow, and he did not seem to think, Bella said, that the picnic would be much fun, but he was greatly amused by the idea of dancing in a half-finished house, and wanted to know where they would find enough ladies for partners; so Mr. Bellairs said there were plenty of partners in the neighbourhood, and pretty ones, too; and Mr. Percy made some speech about being already quite convinced of the beauty of the Cacouna ladies. You know the kind of thing a man would say when Mrs. Bellairs and Bella were there. But Mr. Bellairs told him he had not yet seen a fair specimen; but that there was a little half Spanish girl here who would show him what beauty meant. Mamma, was it not dreadfully stupid of him?" And Lucia, in spite of her indignation, could not restrain a laugh as she looked, half shy, half saucy, into her mother's face.

Mrs. Costello laughed too; but there was as deep a flush on her cheek as on her daughter's, and her heart throbbed painfully.

"Well," she said, "but this *rara avis* was not named?"

"Yes she was. Oh! I can't tell you all; but you know Maurice was there, and Mr. Bellairs told Mr. Percy that he ought to be the best qualified to describe her, because he saw her every day. Then Mr. Percy asked what was her name, and Mr. Bellairs told him. But when Mr. Percy asked Maurice something, he only said, 'Do you believe people *can* be described, Mr. Percy? I don't; and if I did, I should not make a catalogue of a lady's qualities for the benefit of others.'"

"Well done, Lucia, most correctly reported. Who has been telling tales?"

An unsuspected listener stepped out with these words from the dark parlour on to the verandah; but Lucia, springing up at the sound of his voice, flew past him and disappeared.

He came forward, "Don't be angry, Mrs. Costello. I met Margery at the gate, and she sent me in. I assure you I did not hear more than the last sentence; yet, you see I met with a listener's fate."

"I *don't* see it at all. On the contrary, you did hear good of yourself."

"I am glad you think so. Lucia is to be with Mrs. Bellairs to-morrow?"

"Yes. She says at present that she will not, but we shall see."

"I left early, and met Mrs. Bellairs and Miss Latour on the way. They told me they had been here."

Maurice leaned against a pillar of the verandah and was silent, his eyes turned to the door through which Lucia had vanished.

The new guest was much too intimate for Mrs. Costello to dream of "making conversation." She sat quite still looking out.

By this time sunset had entirely faded from the sky, and a few stars were beginning to twinkle faintly; but the rising moon, herself invisible, threw a lovely silver brightness over the river and made a flitting sail glimmer out snowy white as it went silently with a zigzag course up the stream. Between the river and the cottage every object began to be visible with that cold distinctness of outline which belongs to clear moonlight, - every rail of the garden fence, every plant that grew beyond the shadow of the building. A tall acacia-tree which stood on one side waved its graceful leaves in the faint breeze, and caught the light on its long clusters of creamy blossom.

Everything was so peaceful that there seemed, even to herself, a strange discord between the scene within and the heavy pain that sunk deep into her heart this evening - a trembling sense of dread - a passionate yet impotent desire to escape. She pressed her hand upon her heart. The motion roused her from her reverie which indeed had lasted but a minute - one of those long minutes when we in one glance seem to retrace years of the past, and to make a fruitless effort to pierce the veil of the future. She rose, and, bidding her companion "Come in," stepped into the little parlour.

A shaded lamp had been brought in and placed on the table, but the flame was turned down so as to throw only a glimmering light just around it. Mrs. Costello turned it up brightly, and opening the door of the adjoining room, called Lucia, who came, slow and reluctant, at the summons. Maurice pushed forward a little chintz-covered chair into its accustomed place by the table, and looked at the wilful girl as much as to say, "Be reasonable and make friends," but she did not choose to see.

"I can't sit indoors," she said, "it is too hot;" so she went and sat down on the doorstep.

Maurice gave a little impatient sigh, and dropped into a chair which stood opposite to Mrs. Costello, but turned so that without positively looking round, he could see the soft flow of Lucia's muslin dress, and the outline of her head and shoulders.

He had brought, as usual, various odds and ends of news, scraps of European politics or gossip, and morsels of home intelligence, such as women who do not read newspapers like to be told by those who do, and he began to talk about them, but with no interest in what he said; completely preoccupied with that obstinate figure in the doorway. By-and-by, however, the figure changed its position; the head was gradually turned more towards the speakers, and Maurice's as gradually was averted until the two attitudes were completely reversed; he and Mrs. Costello appeared to be engrossed in the subject of a conversation which had now grown animated, while Lucia, from her retreat, stole more and more frequent glances at the visitor. At length she rose softly, and stealing, with the shy step of a child who knows it has been naughty, to her own chair, she slipped into it. A half smile came to Maurice's lips, but he knew his old playfellow's moods too well to take the least notice of her movement, and even when she asked him a question, he simply answered it, and did not even look at her in doing so.

An hour passed. Lucia had entirely recovered from her little fit of sulkiness, and, to the great content of Maurice, was, if possible, even more sweet and winning than usual; but nothing had been said of the next day's plans. When the young man rose to leave, however, Lucia followed him out to the verandah to look at the moonlight.

"We shall have a fine day to-morrow" he said.

"Oh, Maurice," she answered, quickly, as if she had been waiting for the opportunity of speaking, "I am sure mamma does not want me to go, and I would so much rather stay at home. Will you go and tell Mrs. Bellairs in the morning for me?"

"Impossible! Why Lucia, this is a mere fancy of yours."

"Indeed it is not. I am quite in earnest."

"But, my dear child, Mrs. Bellairs has your mother's promise, and I do not see how you can break a positive engagement without better reason."

She stood silent, looking down.

"Are you thinking of that foolish conversation at dinner to-day? I wonder Mrs. Bellairs should have repeated it."

"It was Bella Latour who told me."

"Ah," said Maurice, "I forgot her. Of course it was. Well, at any rate, think no more of it."

"That's very easily said," she answered dolorously "but I do think it's not right," she added with energy, the hot colour rushing into her cheeks, "to speak about one so. It is quite impertinent."

Maurice laughed. "Upon my word I believe very few young ladies would agree with you; however, I assure you it would be giving the enemy an advantage to stay away to-morrow, and I suppose, if I constitute myself your highness's body-guard, you will not be afraid of any more impertinence of the same kind."

He said "Good-night," and ran down the steps. As he passed along the path under the verandah where she stood, she took one of the half-faded roses from her belt and flung it at him. He caught it and with mock gallantry pressed it to his heart; but as he turned through the wicket and along the footpath which led to his home close by, he continued twirling the flower in his fingers. Once it dropped, and without thinking he stooped, and picked it up. He carried it into the house with him, and into his own room, where he laid it down upon his writing-table and forgot it.

Meanwhile, Margery had fastened doors and windows at the cottage, and soon all was silent and dark, except the glimmer of Mrs. Costello's lamp which often burned far into the night. Lucia had been long asleep when her mother stole into her room for that last look which it was her habit to take before she lay down. It was a little white chamber which had been fitted up twelve years before for a child's use; but the child had grown almost into a woman, and there were traces of her tastes and occupations all about. There was a little book-shelf, where Puss in Boots, and Goldsmith's History of England, still kept their places, though the Princess had stepped in between them; there was a drawing of the cottage executed under Maurice's teaching; here was a little work-basket, and there a half-written note. Enough moonlight stole in through the window to show distinctly the lovely dark face resting on the pillow, and surrounded by long hair, glossy, and black as jet. Mrs. Costello stood silently by the bedside.

A kind of shudder passed over her. "She is lovely," she said to herself; "but that terrible beauty! If she had had my pale skin and hair, I should have feared less; but she has nothing of that beauty from me. Yet perhaps it is the best; the whole mental nature may be mine, as the whole physical is -- " Her hand pressed strongly upon her heart. "I have been at peace so long," she went on, "yet I always knew trouble must come again, and through *her*; but if it were only for me, it would be nothing. Now *she* must suffer. I had thought she might escape. But it is the old story, the sins of the fathers -- Can no miseries of mine be enough to free her?"

She turned away into her own room, and shut the door softly, so as not to wake her child; yet firmly, as if she would shut out even that child from all share in her solitary burden.

CHAPTER II

Maurice's prediction of a fine day proved true. At twelve o'clock the weather was as brilliant as possible; the sky blue and clear, the river blue and glittering. The Mermaid, a small steamer, lay in the wharf, gaily decorated with flags; and throngs of people began to gather at the landing and on the deck. Among a group of the most important guests, stood the acknowledged leader of the expedition, the 'Queen of Cacouna,' Mrs. Bellairs. She was talking fast and merrily to everybody in turn, giving an occasional glance to the provision baskets as they were carried on board, and meantime keeping an anxious look-out along the bank of the river, for the appearance of her own little carriage, which ought to have been at the rendezvous long ago.

A very handsome man stood beside her. He was of a type the more striking because specimens of it so rarely found their way in to the fresh, vigorous, hard-working Colonial society. Remarkably tall, yet perfectly proportioned, the roughest backwoodsman might have envied his apparent physical strength; polished in manner to a degree which just, and only just, escaped effeminacy, the most spoiled beauty might have been proud of his homage. At present, however, he stood lazily enough, smiling a little at his hostess' vivacity, exchanging a word or two with her husband, or following the direction of her eyes along the road. At last a cloud of dust appeared. "Here they are, I believe," cried Mrs. Bellairs. "Ah! Maurice, I ought to have sent you, two girls never are to be trusted." Mr. Percy turned round. He was conscious of a little amused curiosity about this Backwoods beauty, and, at hearing this second appeal to Maurice where she was concerned, it occurred to him to look more attentively than he had done before at the person appealed to. They were standing opposite to each other, and they had three attributes in common. Both were tall, both young, and both handsome. Percy was twenty-eight, and looked more than his age. Maurice was twenty-four, and looked less. Percy was fair - his features were admirable - his expression and manner had actually no other fault than that of being too still and languid. Maurice had brown hair, now a little tossed and disordered (for he had been busy all morning on board the boat), a pair of brown eyes of singular beauty, clear and true, and a tolerable set of features, which, like his manner, varied considerably, according to the humour he happened to be in. Percy was a man of the world, understood and respected "les convenances," and never shocked anybody. Maurice knew nothing about the world, and having no more refined rule of conduct than the simple one of right and wrong, which is, perhaps, too lofty for every-day use, he occasionally blundered in his behaviour to people he did not like. At present, indeed, for some reason, by no means clear to himself, he returned the Englishman's glance in anything but a friendly manner.

Bob, the grey pony, trotted down the wharf with his load. Half-a-dozen idlers rushed forwards to help the two girls out of the carriage, and into the boat. Bob marched off in charge of a groom; the paddles began to turn, the flags waved, the band struck up, and the boat moved quickly away down, the stream.

Mrs. Bellairs, relieved from her watch, had sunk into a chair placed on deck, and sent her husband to bring the truants. Maurice remained beside her, and when the rest of the group had a little separated, he bent down and said to her,

"Dear Mrs. Bellairs, don't scold Lucia if the delay is her fault. She had some objection to leaving her mother to-day, and even wanted me to excuse her to you."

"She is a spoiled child," was the answer. "But, however, I will forgive her this once for your sake."

Mr. Percy certainly had not *listened*, but as certainly he had heard this short dialogue. He was rather bored; he did not find Cacouna very amusing, and had not yet found even that last resource of idle men - a woman to flirt with. He was in the very mood to be tempted by anything that promised the slightest distraction, and there was undeniably something irritating in the idea of there being in the neighbourhood one sole and unapproachable beauty, and of that one being given up by common consent to a boy, a mere Canadian boor! Of course he could not understand that no one else could have seen this matter in the light he did; that everybody, or nearly everybody, thought of Maurice and Lucia as near neighbours and old playfellows, and no more. So he felt a very slight stir of indignation, which, in the dearth of other sensations, was not disagreeable. But then probably the girl was quite over-praised; no beauty at all, in fact. People in these outlandish places did not appreciate anything beyond prettiness. "Here she comes."

He almost said the words aloud as Mr. Bellairs brought her forward, but instantly felt disgusted with himself, and stepped back, almost determined not to look at her at all; yet, after all, he was positively curious, and then he must look at her by-and-by. Too late now, - she was talking to Maurice, - always Maurice, - and had her back completely turned; there was nothing visible but the outline of a tall slight figure. "Not ungraceful, certainly; but Mrs. Bellairs is graceful, and Miss Latour not bad; it must be walking so much. What a gorilla that fellow looks! The women here are decidedly better than the men."

His soliloquy stopped short. Lucia had turned to look at something, and their eyes met. A most lovely crimson flush rushed to her cheeks, and gave her face the only beauty it generally wanted; she instantly turned away again, but Mr. Percy's meditations remained suspended. A few minutes afterwards he walked away to the other end of the boat, and

Lucia felt relieved when she caught sight of his tall figure towering among a cloud of muslins and feathers, quite out of hearing. Maurice brought her a stool, and she sat peaceably leaning against the bulwarks, and enjoying the bright day and swift motion, until they reached the small woody island where the party were to dine.

The boat was soon deserted, and the gentlemen occupied themselves in arranging the hampers and packages near to the place chosen for dinner. Then three or four of the most capable being left in charge of the preparations, the rest dispersed in all directions until they should be summoned to their meal.

A number of the young girls, under the guidance of Bella Latour, crossed the island to the edge of a tiny bay, where they stained their fingers with wild strawberries, and washed them in the river. They collected enough fruit to fill all the large leaves they could find, and then sat down under the shade of a tree to enjoy their spoil and "a good talk." This highest of feminine delights, however, was not left uninterrupted. Half-a-dozen gentlemen made their appearance, carrying bows, arrows, targets, etc., and seeking a good place for an impromptu archery-ground. Everybody sprang up, the ground was chosen, bows and arrows distributed, and shouts of laughter began to follow each shot of the unpractised archers. Of the whole group, Bella, Lucia, and May Anderson, a little yellow-haired Scotch girl, were the only ones who had even attempted to shoot before. May was the first whose arrow touched the target at all, and her success was followed by other failures, until Lucia's turn came. Lucia, to confess the truth, was a little out of humour still. She was not enjoying herself at all, though it would have puzzled her to say why, and she took the bow that was offered her, and stepped forward to her place in the laziest way imaginable. A considerable number of lookers-on had by this time gathered round the clear space, and just as she was carelessly raising her bow she caught sight of Mrs. Bellairs' grey cloak, and Mr. Percy's tall figure beside it.

"The fop!" she said to herself. "He thinks we are all half savages," and with the energy of her ill-humour she suddenly changed her attitude, drew her bow, and sent her arrow straight to the centre.

Of course it was all chance. Nobody was more astonished than herself, but at any rate it was a success, and success is always agreeable. Before she had time to peril her new reputation by a second trial, the boat-bell rung to announce dinner, and everybody returned to the place which had been chosen for the meal.

All picnics have a strong family likeness: even in Canada there is nothing new in them. Mr. Percy hated picnics, and found this one neither more nor less stupid than usual. The slight fillip which Lucia had innocently given to his bored faculties, soon subsided. He sat near her at dinner, and thought her stupid; he noticed too that she wore her hat badly, and had a very countrified air, "of course."

The boat returned up the river much more slowly than it had gone down. The elder people were tired, and the younger ones began to think of the evening, and to reserve themselves for it. The band played at intervals, with long pauses, as if the musicians were tired too. Mrs. Bellairs had resumed her chair on deck, but some of the elder ladies were gathered round her; Bella and Lucia sat together in one corner. Dr. Morton, the most desirable *parti* in Cacouna, was literally, as well as figuratively, at Bella's feet, and Maurice leaned on the railing beside them. Mr. Percy was happier than he had been all day; he had been taken possession of by a pretty young matron - an Englishwoman, who still talked of "home," and they had found out some mutual acquaintance, of whom she was eager to hear news. Yet he was not too much engrossed to perceive the group opposite to him, or even to keep up a kind of half-conscious surveillance over them. At the landing the party dispersed, almost all to meet again in the evening at the unfinished house, which had been appropriated for a ball-room. Mrs. Bellairs drove her sister and Lucia home, leaving

Mr. Bellairs and Mr. Percy to follow; and when they arrived, the ladies had shut themselves up in their rooms, to drink tea and rest before dressing.

At nine o'clock, while Mr. Percy was finishing his toilette, his host knocked at the door. "Are you ready?" he asked. "Elise was anxious to see the rooms before anybody arrived, so she and the girls are gone some time ago with Maurice Leigh."

"Gone! Why, Bellairs, what hours *do* people keep in Canada?"

"In Cacouna they keep reasonable ones, my good cousin; we begin to dance at nine and finish soon after twelve. That accounts for the young people being young. But come, if you are ready."

The house where the dance was to take place stood on a slight elevation, so that its unglazed windows, blazing with light, shone out conspicuously and lighted the approaching guests as they wound their way among the rough heaps of mortar, planks, and various *debris* left by the workmen. The two gentlemen made their way readily to the open door, and stepped at once into full view of the ball-room.

It was a space of about fifty feet long and thirty wide, running all across the house from back to front. Chandeliers of most primitive construction had been hung from the roof, and so skilfully decked with green that the rough splinters of wood which formed them were completely hidden. Flags and garlands ornamented the rough brick walls, and with plenty of light and flowers, and no small amount of taste and skill, the volunteer decorators had in fact succeeded in making out of rather unpromising materials, a very gay and brilliant-looking saloon.

A small space near the door had been railed off, and served as a passage to the dressing-rooms, from which sounds of voices and laughter came merrily, though the ball-room itself was at present quite empty.

"Your neighbours are not quite so punctual as you would have me believe," said Mr. Percy; "there is not even a fiddler visible."

At that moment Mrs. Bellairs put her head out of a dressing-room. "Oh, William!" she said, "I'm so glad you are come. Have you seen Maurice or Henry Scott?"

"No indeed. Where are your fiddlers?"

"Just what I want to know. When we came they had not arrived, and Henry was gone to look for them. Maurice only waited a few minutes, and finding they did not come, he went too. What shall we do?"

"Wait, I suppose. They are sure to be here immediately. I only hope they will arrive tolerably sober."

Mrs. Bellairs shrugged her shoulders and retreated. Mr. Percy smiled rather contemptuously.

"Do these accidents often happen?" he asked.

"Dear me! no. I never knew anything to go wrong where Elise had the management, before. But I must go and look if they are coming."

He hurried out, but scarcely passed the doorway when the lost musicians appeared, under the guidance of Maurice and Henry Scott. They were not, perhaps, quite beyond suspicion as to sobriety, but there was no fear of their being unable to do their duty reasonably well. The happy news of their arrival being made known by the commencement of a vigorous tuning, the doors of the dressing-rooms opened, and the ball-room began to fill.

The common opinion of Cacouna had undoubtedly been that Mr. Percy - the Honourable Edward Percy, whose name was in the Peerage - would dance the first quadrille with Mrs. Bellairs.

But sovereigns are permitted to be capricious, especially female ones, and the Queen of Cacouna was not above the weaknesses of her class. Perhaps Mr. Percy - who was certainly bored himself - bored her a little. At any rate she signified her intention of bestowing her hand upon an elderly gentleman, the owner of the house, to whom, as she said, they were so much indebted for his kindness in allowing them to metamorphose it as they had done.

The gentleman, thus left at liberty to choose his own partner, found his eyes turning naturally to Lucia; but before he had quite made up his mind, Maurice came up to her.

"Lucia," he said, "I shall be obliged to give up my quadrille. It is a great nuisance; but keep the next for me, will you not?"

She nodded and smiled, and he hurried off.

Mr. Percy still stood undecided. His cousin touched him on the shoulder, "Are not you going to dance?" he asked.

"I suppose so," with the slightest possible shrug. "Miss Costello, if you are disengaged, will you dance this quadrille with me?"

Lucia turned when he spoke. The same deep crimson flush came to her face as when their eyes had first met that morning. She felt angry with him for asking her, and with Maurice for having left her free. She longed to say to him some of the civil impertinences women can use to men they dislike, but she was too great a novice, and found no better expedient than to accept the invitation as coolly as it was given. Probably, however, Mr. Percy attributed her blush to a cause very different from its real one; or else there was something soothing and agreeable in finding himself in possession of incomparably the prettiest partner in the room, for he began almost immediately to feel less bored, and positively roused himself to the extent of making some exertion to please his reluctant companion.

Mrs. Harry Coghill

Now, it was all very well for Lucia to be cross, and to nurse her crossness to the last possible minute, but a girl of sixteen, however pretty and however spoiled, is not generally gifted with sufficient strength of mind or badness of temper, to remain quite insensible to the good qualities of a handsome man, who evidently wishes to make himself agreeable to her. When the man in question is the lion of the day, probably his success becomes inevitable; at all events, Lucia gradually recovered her good humour, and kept up her part of the broken chat possible under the circumstances, with enough grace and spirit to give to her extraordinary beauty the last crowning charm which Percy had not, until then, found in it.

Thus they finished their quadrille in good humour with each other, but as they left their place to rejoin Mrs. Bellairs, Maurice Leigh came into the room by a side door. The sight of him reminded Mr. Percy of the short dialogue he had heard.

"You are engaged for the next quadrille, are you not?" he asked Lucia.

"Yes, to Maurice. I promised it to him instead of the first."

"You were to have danced this one with him, then?"

She laughed. "It is a childish arrangement of ours," she said; "we agreed, long ago, always to dance the first quadrille together, and everybody knows of it, so no one asks me for that."

"I wonder at his being willing to miss his privilege to-night; you must be very indulgent, not to punish him."

"Oh! you know he is acting as a kind of steward to-night and has so many things to do. It was not his fault."

"And you would have waited patiently for him?"

"Patiently? I don't know. Certainly I should have waited, for no one but a stranger would have asked me to dance."

"I hope, however, you forgive me."

They had reached Mrs. Bellair's, and she only answered by a smile as she sat down. A minute after, she was carried off by another partner, and Mr. Percy took possession of the vacant place.

The evening passed on. At the end of it, Mr. Percy, shut up in his own room, surprised himself in the midst of a reverie the subject of which was Lucia Costello; he actually found himself comparing her with a certain Lady Adeliza Weymouth, of whom he had been supposed to be *epris* the season before. But then Lady Adeliza had no particular claim to beauty; she was "distinguished" and of a powerful family; as for Lucia, on the other hand, she was -- There! it was no use going off into that question. A great deal more sense to go to bed.

Meantime Lucia, under Maurice's escort, was on her way home. They had started, talking gaily enough, but before half the distance was passed they grew silent.

After a long pause Maurice asked, "Are you very tired?"

Lucia's meditation had carried her so far away that she started at the sound of his voice.

"Tired? oh, no! At least not very much."

"And you have enjoyed the day after all?"

"Pretty well. Not much, I think."

"I thought you looked happy enough this evening. Come, confess you are glad you did not stay at home."

"Indeed, I will not; mamma, I am sure, wished me to stay?"

"Yet she made you come."

"Yes, because she thought I wanted to do so. Maurice, do you think she looks ill?"

"No, I have not noticed it. Does she complain?"

"Mamma complain! A thing she *never* does. But it seems to me that something is different. I can't tell what. She goes out less than ever, and seems to dislike my leaving her." Lucia longed to say, "She has some trouble; some heavy anxiety; can you guess what it is?" but she had an instinctive consciousness, that even to this dear and tried friend, she ought not to speak of a subject on which Mrs. Costello was invariably silent. Even to herself, a certain darkness hung over her mother's past life; there were years of it of which she felt utterly ignorant. Whatever was the cloud of the present, it might be connected with the recollections of those years; this thought checked her even while she spoke.

Whether Maurice had any similar reason for reticence or not, he only said, "I do not think she would hide anything from you which need give you uneasiness. I advise you not to torment yourself causelessly."

"I am not tormenting myself; but I think yours is a miserable plan. You would have people feel no sympathy for the troubles of others, unless they can be paraded in so many words."

"Decidedly you must be very tired, or you would take the trouble to understand me better."

He put down his whip, to draw her cloak more closely round her, for the dewy night air was chill, but she pushed it away.

"I am quite warm, thank you. How long the road seems to-night! Shall we ever be at home?"

"We are almost there. See, that is your own acacia-tree."

"I am so glad. Don't turn up the lane. I can run up there perfectly well by myself."

"Indeed you will not. Sit still, if you please."

"How tiresome you are, Maurice! You treat me just as if I were a baby."

"Do I? A bad habit, I suppose. I will try to cure myself."

His tone was so quiet, so free from either ridicule or anger, that she grew more impatient still.

"Now pray do let me get out. I can see Mr. Leigh's light burning still, as well as mamma's. They must both be tired of waiting. Why does your father always sit up for you, Maurice? Is he afraid to trust you?"

"Lucia!" His tone was angry now, and silenced her. In another minute they stopped at the gate of the cottage.

Mrs. Costello had heard the sound of their wheels, and instantly opened the door. Lucia's half-formed intention of making some kind of apology for her petulance, had no time to ripen. Maurice helped her down without speaking, bade her good night, exchanged a word or two with her mother, and drove slowly away again.

Mother and daughter went in together to Lucia's room; but Mrs. Costello, noticing that her child looked pale and weary, left her almost immediately. Lucia instantly flew to the window. The farmhouse where Mr. Leigh and Maurice lived was so near that the lights in its different windows could be plainly distinguished. After a moment, the one which had been burning steadily as they passed the house, flickered suddenly, disappeared, and then, shone more brightly through the opening door.

"He is at home," said Lucia to herself. "Poor Maurice, how

good he is! What on earth made me so cross?"

She continued to watch. Presently the light which had returned to the sitting-room vanished altogether, and a fainter gleam stole out from what she knew to be the window of Maurice's room. She said "Good-night" softly, as if he could hear her, dropped her curtain, and was soon fast asleep.

That night Mrs. Costello's lamp was extinguished long before Maurice's. Tired and dispirited, he had seated himself before his little writing-table, and given himself up to a dream of no pleasant kind. It was so completely the habit of his life to think of Lucia that it would have been strange if her image had not been prominent in his meditations; but to-night for the first time he tried to get rid of this image. He was used to her whims and changing moods, to her waywardness and occasional tyranny. When he was a boy they had often quarrelled, and taxed the efforts of his sister Alice, Lucia's inseparable friend, to reconcile them; but since his long absence at college, and, above all, since Alice's death, they had ceased to torment each other. The relations of master and pupil had been added to those of playfellows, and their intercourse had run on so smoothly that until to-night Maurice had never known his charge's full power to irritate him. Like most persons of steady and equable temperament, he felt deeply annoyed, even humiliated, by having been surprised into impatience and anger; he was doubly displeased with himself and with Lucia. Yet, as he thought of her his mood softened; she was only a child, and would be good to-morrow. But then she could not always be a child - a girl of sixteen ought to be beginning to be reasonable; and then she did not look such a child. He had been struck by that idea at one particular moment of this very evening. It was when he had returned to the ball-room at the close of the first quadrille, and had met Lucia walking up the room with Mr. Percy. They had been talking together with animation; Lucia was a little flushed, and looking more lovely than usual. Mr. Percy, for his part, appeared to have forgotten his cool, almost supercilious manner, and to be occupied more with her than with himself.

Maurice felt his cheek grow red as he recalled the picture. He moved impatiently, and in doing so, displaced some loose papers, which slipped to the ground. In stooping to gather them up, his hand touched a dead flower, which had fallen with them. It was Lucia's rose. He was just about to throw it down again, when his hand stopped. "She spoke of something different," he muttered; "are the old times coming to an end, I wonder? Times *must* change, I suppose." He sighed, and instead of throwing the rose away, he slipped it into an envelope and locked it into his desk.

Mrs. Harry Coghill

CHAPTER III

The Honourable Edward Percy was the younger son of the Earl of Lastingham, and might therefore be readily excused if he considered himself a person of some importance in a country where a baronetcy is the highest hereditary dignity, and where many of the existing "honourables" began life as country storekeepers or schoolmasters. It is true that in his own proper orbit, this luminary appeared but a star of small magnitude, his handsome person and agreeable qualities making slight compensation for a want of fortune which he had always considered a special hardship in his own case; regarding himself as admirably fitted by nature for spending money, and knowing by experience that his abilities were totally inadequate to saving it. His family was not rich; so far from it, indeed, that the great object of the Earl had been to marry his daughters like Harpagon's "sans dot," a task which was not yet satisfactorily accomplished; and all he had been able to do for his younger son, had been to use the very small political influence he possessed, to start him in life as an *attache*.

So the young man had seen various Courts, and improved his French and German; and at nearly thirty years of age he had begun to think that it was time to take another step in life.

This idea was strengthened by a short conversation with his father. He had paid a visit to Lastingham with the double object of attending the marriage of one of his sisters, and of trying to persuade the Earl to pay some inconvenient debts.

But the moment he mentioned, with due caution, this second reason for his arrival, he found it a hopeless cause. He represented that his income was small, and his prospects of advancement extremely slender.

"Marry," said the Earl.

"Thank you. I would rather not. I want to get rid of my incumbrances, not to increase them."

"Marry," repeated the Earl.

"But whom?" asked his son, staggered by this oracular response.

"Miss Drummond."

"She's fifty, at least."

"And has a hundred thousand pounds."

"She would not have me."

"You are growing modest."

"Not in that respect. She has refused half-a-dozen offers every season for the last twenty years."

"Miss Pelham?"

"What would be the use of that?"

"Family interest."

"Too many sons in the way."

"Lady Adeliza Weymouth?"

Percy made a slight grimace.

"She is a year older than I am, and has a red nose; otherwise -- "

"You had better think of it, at any rate," said the Earl, "and try if she will have you. Depend upon it, a sensible marriage is the best thing for you."

On which advice the son had dutifully acted. Fortune favoured him so far as to give him opportunities of cultivating the good graces of Lady Adeliza, and matters appeared to be going on prosperously. It seemed, however, that either the gentleman found wooing in earnest to be a more fatiguing business than he had anticipated, or he thought that a short absence might increase the chances in his favour, for on the slightest possible pretence of being sent out by Government he started off one day for Canada.

Now, when Lord Lastingham had spoken so wisely about a sensible marriage, he had been drawing lessons from his own experience. The late Countess had been a very charming woman, of good family, but, like her daughters, "sans dot;" and the infatuation which caused so imprudent a connection not having lasted beyond the first year of matrimony, the Earl had had plenty of time to repent and to calculate, over and over again, how different the fortunes of his house might have been, had he acted, himself, upon the principles he recommended to his son. It was with some displeasure that he heard Edward's intention of giving up, for a while, his pursuit of a desirable bride, and this displeasure was not lessened by hearing that the truant intended prolonging his expedition, for the purpose of visiting his mother's nephew, William Bellairs.

The journey, however, was made without any opposition on the Earl's part. Mr. Percy spent a few weeks in Quebec, then the seat of Government, and travelling slowly westward arrived finally at his cousin's house at Cacouna. Mr. Bellairs was a barrister in good practice; his pretty wife, a Frenchwoman by descent, had brought him a fortune of considerable amount for the colonies, and knew how to make his house sufficiently attractive. Both received their English relative with hearty hospitality, and thus it happened that the even current of Cacouna society was disturbed by the appearance of a visitor important enough to be a centre of attraction.

The morning after the picnic Mr. Bellairs proposed to his guest that they should drive along the river-bank to some rapids a few miles distant, which formed one of the objects to which visitors to Cacouna were in the habit of making pilgrimages. They went accordingly, in a light waggon, and having duly admired the rapids, and the surrounding scenery, started for home. Their way led past the Leighs' house and the end of the lane leading to Mrs. Costello's. Mr. Bellairs pointed them both out to his companion.

"Do you see that cottage close to the river? That is the nest of the prettiest bird in Cacouna; and in this long white house to the right lives my most hopeful pupil and my wife's right hand, Maurice Leigh."

"Miss Costello told me they were near neighbours," said Mr. Percy. "Has she no father or brother, that she seems to be so much the property of this pupil of yours?"

"No, indeed, poor girl! Her father died, I believe, when she was an infant. Mrs. Costello came here twelve years ago, a widow, with this one child."

"Is young Leigh any relation?"

Mr. Bellairs laughed. "Not at present certainly, though I have thought it would come to that by-and-by. It is only a case of devoted friendship. Alice Leigh, Maurice's sister, and Lucia used to be always together; but poor Alice died, and I suppose Maurice felt bound to make up to Lucia for the loss."

"Who or what are the Leighs then? It is a queer-looking place."

"Mr. Leigh is an Englishman; he came out here many years ago with a young wife; she is dead and so are all her children except Maurice. Father and son live there together alone."

"I don't of course pretend to know how you manage such things in Canada, but it appears to me that a beautiful girl, like Miss Costello, might expect a better match, at least if one is to judge of the Leighs by their house."

"I am not sure that we should call Maurice a bad match for any girl. With a fair amount of brains, and a great capacity for work, he would be sure to get on in a country like ours, even if he were less thoroughly a good fellow. He has but two faults; he is too scrupulous about trifles, and a little too Quixotic in his ideas about women. However, my wife will never let me say that."

The subject did not interest Mr. Percy; he began to ask questions about something else, and they soon after reached home. Later in the day Mrs. Bellairs met him coming in extremely bored from her husband's office.

"I am going to pay some visits," she said, "are you disposed to go with me?"

"Most thankfully," he answered. "I have been listening to half-a-dozen cases of trespass, not a single word of which I could understand. It will be doing me the greatest kindness to take me into civilized society."

"I thought," she said laughing, "that you came to the backwoods to escape civilized society."

"If I did," he replied, handing her into the pony-carriage, "it is quite clear that I made a happy mistake."

"I am going first," she said, as soon as Bob was fairly in motion, "to the Parsonage. Mr. and Mrs. Bayne were to have been with us yesterday, but one of the children was ill, and I must inquire after it."

Mr. Percy's politeness just enabled him to suppress a groan. He had seen Mrs. Bayne once, and not been delighted, - and a sick child! However, duty before all. They stopped at the gate of the Parsonage. It was a tolerably large house, standing on a sloping lawn, overlooking the river on one side and the little town on the other; but the lawn was entered only by a wicket, so that Bob had to be fastened to the railing, while the visitors walked up to the house.

The moment they were seen approaching three or four children ran out of the hall, where they were playing, and fell upon Mrs. Bellairs.

"Don't eat me," she cried, kissing them all in turn. "Which is the invalid? Where is mamma?"

"It was Nina," shouted a chorus; "she fell into the river. Mamma's in the house."

By this time they had reached the door, and Mrs. Bayne appeared, having been attracted by their voices. She was a little woman, thin and worn, so worn indeed, by many children and many cares, that she looked fifty instead of thirty-five. She had on a faded dress, and her collar and cuffs had been soiled and crumpled by the attacks of her younger boys and girls, especially the fat baby she held in her arms; but she had long ago ceased to be embarrassed by the shabbiness of her toilette, or the inevitable disorder of her sitting-room. She found seats for her guests, and to do so pushed into the background the baby's cradle and an old easy-chair, in which the luckless Nina was sitting bundled up in shawls.

Mrs. Bellairs took the baby, which instantly became absorbed in trying to pull out the long feather of her hat, drew her chair close to the little invalid, and began to inquire into the accident. Mr. Percy, determined to make the best of his circumstances, endeavoured to make friends with the heir of the house, a sturdy boy of nine or ten, but as the young gentleman declined to do anything, except put his finger in his mouth and stare, he found himself without other occupation than that of listening to the conversation of the two ladies.

"It was the night before last," Mrs. Bayne was saying; "they were playing on the bank, and Miss Nina chose to climb into a tree that overhangs the river. Of course when she got up, the most natural thing in the world was that she should slip down again, but unluckily she did not fall on the grass, but into the water."

Mrs. Bellairs shuddered. "What an awful risk!"

"My dear, they are always running risks. I am sure among the seven there is always one in danger."

"Well?"

"Well, Charlie ran to the study to his papa, and when Mr. Bayne went out, there was Nina, who had been partly stunned by her fall, beginning to float away with the current. Fortunately she had fallen in so near the edge that the water was very shallow, and if she had been in possession of her senses, she might have dragged herself out I dare say; but, you know, the current is very strong, and her papa had to get into the river a little lower down and catch her as she was passing."

"And she was insensible?"

"Not quite when they brought her in, but then unluckily her wetting brought on ague again, and she was shivering all night."

"Poor Nina!" and Mrs. Bellairs turned to the miserable pale child, who looked as if another shivering fit were coming on. "You must make haste and get better, and come and stay with Flo for a while. We never have ague."

"You are fortunate," sighed Mrs. Bayne. "I wish that wretched swamp *could* be done something to."

"So do I, with all my heart. I must tease William into giving the people no rest until they do it."

"You will be doing us and our poor neighbours at the shanties no small service. Ague is dreadfully bad there just now."

A frantic pull at Mrs. Bellairs' hat from the baby interrupted the conversation, and the visitors rose to go.

When they were once more on the road Mrs. Bellairs turned laughingly to her companion, "Tell me," she said, "don't you agree with me that a visit to the Parsonage furnishes a tolerably strong argument in favour of a clergy such as the Roman Catholic?"

"That is, an unmarried one? Are many of your clergymen's wives like Mrs. Bayne?"

"If you mean are they worn out, overworked women? Yes, I believe so. How can they help it indeed, when one hundred a year is a very ordinary amount for a clergyman's income?"

Mr. Percy shrugged his shoulders. "I agree with you entirely. No man ought to marry under those circumstances. But I wish you would enlighten me on one point, - what are shanties?"

"Log-houses of the roughest possible kind, such as are built in the woods for the gangs of lumberers; that is, you know, the men who cut down the trees and prepare them for shipping."

"But Mrs. Bayne said something about shanties near here."

"Yes. Beyond their house, there lies, along the river, a swamp of no great extent, which ought to have been drained long ago. Beyond that, on the edge of the bush, is a large saw-mill, and the families of the men employed at this mill live in shanties close by. Every spring and autumn the sickness among them is terrible, and sometimes there are bad cases all through the summer. But you may imagine what it is among those people in their wretched damp, unventilated homes, when even the Baynes suffer as poor little Nina is doing now, and did most of the spring."

"Delightful country!" said Mr. Percy, "and people positively like to live here."

"Yes!" replied Mrs. Bellairs, with spirit, "and with good cause. As for what I have been telling you, has not England been quite as bad? I have heard that in Lincolnshire, and the adjoining counties, not a lifetime ago, ague was as prevalent as in our worst districts. The same means which destroyed it there, will do so here; the work is half accomplished already, for this very road on which we are driving was, twenty years ago, little better than a bog along which it was not safe for a horse to pass."

"Wonderful energy your people must have, certainly. Where are we going next?"

Mrs. Bellairs was provoked. She was an ardent lover of her country; and to talk of its advantages and disadvantages with an interested companion was to her a keen pleasure; the intense indifference of Mr. Percy's reply, therefore, made her regard him for a moment with anything but goodwill. She gave Bob a sharp "flick" with her whip, and paused a minute before answering; when she did speak, it was with a little malice.

"I suppose you have not yet had time to call on Maurice Leigh? I can take you there now if you like. I often go to see old Mr. Leigh."

"Thank you. I saw young Leigh just now at William's office."

"I am going to the Cottage then, that is, Mrs. Costello's."

They were almost at the turning of the lane as she spoke, and directly after came in sight of the pretty low house, standing in a perfect nest of green. They stopped at the gate; and Margery, a decent middle-aged woman, immediately came out to open it. She took hold of the pony like an old acquaintance, and fastened him to a post in such a way that he could amuse himself by nibbling the grass which grew along the little-frequented path; then smoothing down her white apron, ushered the visitors into the parlour. The room was very dark, the Venetian shutters being closed and blinds drawn down to keep out the glare and heat of the day, but the flicker of a white dress on the verandah showed where the two ladies were to be found. Mrs. Bellairs stepped out, and was greeted by a cry of delight from Lucia.

"Oh, you are good! Is Bella here?"

"Bella is gone to the Scotts', but Mr. Percy is with me."

Lucia grew demure instantly, as the second guest came forward. "Mamma is there," she said, and made room for them to pass along the verandah.

Mrs. Bellairs presented her companion to her friend, and more chairs were brought out, that the new-comers might enjoy the cool breeze and shade. Mr. Percy might have preferred a seat near Lucia; fortune, however, placed him beside her mother, and, like a wise man, he applied himself to make the best of his position. How little trouble this cost him he did not discover until afterwards; but, in fact, he had rarely met with a woman who, by her own personal qualities, was so well fitted to inspire feelings of both friendship and respect as this quiet undemonstrative Mrs. Costello.

Lucia and Mrs. Bellairs meantime had discussed yesterday and its doings, and passed to other plans of amusement - rides, drives, and fishing parties. Time passed, as pleasant times often do, without anything particular being said or done, to mark its flight, and the call had lasted nearly an hour before it came to a close.

When it did, permission had been wrung from Mrs. Costello for Lucia to spend a long day with Mrs. Bellairs, at a farm in the country, which belonged, jointly, to her and her sister. The whole family were to drive out from Cacouna in the morning, calling for Lucia, and were to bring her back in the evening.

"Let us go this way," said Mrs. Bellairs, turning to the steps which led down into the garden. Lucia followed her. "You have not seen my new roses," she said. "Do come and look at them."

"Bella told me you had some fine ones," answered Mrs. Bellairs, "but I have not patience to look at my neighbours' flowers this year, mine have been such a failure."

"These certainly are not a failure," said Mr. Percy, as they reached a bed of beautiful roses in full bloom. "Have you any flower-shows in Canada? You ought to exhibit, Miss Costello."

Lucia laughed. "What chance should I have? They say an amateur never can compete with a professed gardener, and ours is all amateur work."

"Is it possible? Do you mean to say that you do actually cultivate your flowers with your own hands?"

"Certainly, with a little help from my friends." She was about to say "from Maurice," but changed the phrase. "If you saw me at work here in the mornings, you would at least give me credit for trying to cultivate them."

"Should I? You tempt me to take a peep into your Eden some morning when you are gardening."

"Pray don't," she answered, laughing. "The effects would be too dreadful."

"What would they be?"

"The moment you caught sight of my working costume you would be seized with such a horror of Backwoods manners and customs that you would fly, not only from Cacouna, but from Canada, at the expense of I do not know what business of State."

"I wonder why you, and so many of your neighbours, seem to think of an Englishman as if he were a fine lady. That has not generally been the character of the race."

Lucia felt inclined to say, "We do not think so of all Englishmen;" but she held her tongue. Either intentionally, or by accident, Mr. Percy had stood, during this short dialogue, in such a manner as to prevent her from following Mrs. Bellairs when she turned back from the rose-bed; and, in spite of her sauciness, she was too shy to make any effort to pass. He moved a little now, and she had half escaped, when he said, "I have not seen a really beautiful rose in Canada till now; may I have one?"

She was obliged to go back and gather one of her pet flowers for him; then choosing another for Mrs. Bellairs, she carried it to her friend, who, by this time had reached the pony-carriage, and was just taking her seat.

Lucia gave her the rose, and then remained standing by the little gate until Bob's head was turned towards home, when his mistress suddenly checked him.

"Oh! Lucia," she called out, "I had nearly forgotten; will you give Maurice a message for me?"

"Yes, if I see him," and for the first time in her life, Lucia blushed at Maurice's name. But then Mr. Percy was looking at her.

"'If you see him,'" laughed Mrs. Bellairs "tell him, please, that I want him to pay me a little visit to-morrow morning before he goes to the office. Say that it is very important and will only detain him a few minutes."

"Very well."

"Mind you don't forget. Good-bye."

"'Maurice,' 'Maurice,'" said Lucia, pettishly to herself. "It seems as if there was no one in the world but Maurice."

There was an odd coincidence at that moment between Lucia's thoughts and Mr. Percy's; neither, however, said anything about them to their companions.

Mrs. Costello was quietly knitting, when her daughter came slowly back, up the steps of the verandah, but Lucia was too restless and dissatisfied to sit down. She wanted something, and had not the least idea what. At last, she began to think that staying at home all day had made her feel so cross and uncomfortable.

"Mamma, do come for a walk," she said, putting her arm round her mother. "Come, I am tired of the house."

"You are tired, darling, I believe. Remember how late you were last night. But it is tea-time now."

"Oh, what a nuisance! I can go out afterwards, though."

"Yes, I dare say Maurice will walk with you."

"Mamma, I think I shall go to bed."

"In the meantime sit down here and talk to me."

She dropped down on the floor, and laid her head on her mother's lap.

"Talk to me, mamma. Talk about England."

An old, old theme. Mother and daughter had talked about England, the far-away Mother Land, many many hours full of pleasure to both; to one the subject had all the enchantment of a fairy tale, to the other of the tenderest and sweetest recollections. Lucia had heard, over and over again, each detail of the landscape, each incident in the history, of her mother's birthplace; she knew the gentle invalid mistress and the kind stern master, her grandfather and grandmother; she had loved to gather into her garden the flowers which had grown about the grey walls of the old house by the Dee; the one wish she had cherished from a child was to see with living eyes all that was so familiar to her fancy. But to-day, though she said, "Talk about England," it was not of all this she wished to hear; and an instinctive feeling that it was not, kept Mrs. Costello from speaking. She laid her hand gently upon her child's head and remained silent. Lucia was silent, also. She wanted her mother to talk, yet hesitated to ask her the questions she wanted answered. At last she said abruptly,

"Mamma, did you *ever* gossip?"

Mrs. Costello laughed.

"Do you think I never do now, then? I am afraid I cannot say as much for myself."

"I never hear you. But when you were a girl, you must have heard things about people."

"No doubt I did. And I suppose that, as I lived in almost as quiet a neighbourhood as this, I must have been curious and interested about a new-comer, much as you are."

Lucia turned her head a little, and smiled to herself.

"And then?" she said.

"Then most likely I asked questions, and found out all I could about the new-comer, which, I suppose, you have been doing about Mr. Percy. Bella Latour ought to be a good authority."

"I have not asked any questions. I thought perhaps you might know something about him, or at least about his family."

"About him I certainly know nothing. It is twenty years since I left England, and he would then be only a child. His father I have seen two or three times. Mr. Percy resembles him extremely."

"Was he a handsome man, then?"

"Very handsome. And Lady Lastingham was said to be a most beautiful woman."

"You never saw her?"

"No, she died young. Lord Lastingham married her, as people said, for love; that is to say, her great beauty tempted him. They were very poor, and he was not of a character to bear poverty. She was good and amiable, but he wearied of her, and scarcely pretended to feel her death as a loss."

"Oh! mamma, how could that be possible? if he married her for love?"

"For what he called love, at least. There are men, my child, and perhaps women also, whose only kind of love is a fancy, like a child's for a toy. They see something which attracts them; they try their utmost to obtain it. If they fail, they soon forget their disappointment; if they succeed, they are delighted for the moment, until, the novelty having worn off, they discover that they have paid too dearly for their gratification, and throw aside their new possession in disgust."

Mrs. Costello spoke earnestly, and with a kind of suppressed passion. It seemed as if her words had an application beyond Lucia's knowledge; yet they awed her strangely. Could they be true? Who then could be trusted? for according to her mother's story, Lord Lastingham had not merely deceived his wife, he had deceived himself also, with this counterfeit love. She fell into a reverie, which lasted till the noise of cups and saucers, as Margery brought in tea, put it to flight.

CHAPTER IV

Two or three weeks passed. The inhabitants of Cacouna had grown accustomed to the sight of Mr. Percy's tall figure, as he lounged from his cousin's house to his office, or rode and drove with Mrs. Bellairs. From different causes, the project of spending the day at the farm, as well as some other schemes of amusement, had been deferred, and, with one or two exceptions, all was going on as usual. The most notable of these exceptions was in the life at the cottage, formerly so calm, so regular, so smooth in its current. Now a change had crept over both mother and daughter, and the very atmosphere of the house seemed to have changed with them.

In Lucia, even a casual visitor would have remarked the difference. Her beauty seemed suddenly to have burst from bud into blossom; her childishness of manner had almost left her; her voice, especially in singing, had grown more full and musical.

In Mrs. Costello, the change was the reverse of all this. Mrs. Bellairs and Maurice Leigh, the two people, who, except her daughter, loved her best, grieved over her unrested, pallid face, and noticed that her soft brown hair had more and more visible streaks of grey. They thought her ill, and each had said so, but she answered so positively that nothing was the matter, that they were unable to do more than seem to accept her assurances. But to Lucia, when, with a tenderness which seemed to have grown both deeper and more fitful, she would implore to be told the cause of such evident suffering, Mrs.

Costello gave a different answer.

"I have told our friends the truth," she said; "I am not ill in body, but a little anxious and disturbed in mind. Have patience for a while, my darling, the time for you to share all my thoughts is, I fear, not far distant."

So Lucia waited, too full of life and happiness herself to be much troubled even by the shadow resting on her mother, and growing daily more absorbed in a strange new delight of her own - seeing all things through a new medium, and filling her heart too full of the joy of the present, to leave room in it for one grave fear of the future.

Wonderful alchemy of the imagination, which can draw from a nature ignoble, and altogether earthly, nourishment for dreams so sweet and so sunny! Lucia's fancy had made for her a picture, such as most girls make for themselves once in their lives, and the portrait was as unfaithful as the original himself could have desired. Mr. Percy had become almost a daily visitor at the Cottage. Attracted by Lucia's beauty, he came, as he would have said, had he spoken frankly, to amuse himself during a dull visit, with no thought but that of entertaining himself and her for the moment. But, in fact, the magnet had more power over him than he knew; he came, because, without a much stronger effort of self-denial than was possible to him, he could not stay away. And though he thought himself free, Lucia had in her heart an unacknowledged sense of power over him; the old ability to torment, which she had so often exercised on Maurice in mere girlish playfulness. Once or twice she had purposely exerted this power over her new acquaintance, but not with her old carelessness; too deeply interested in the question of how far it extended, she used it with trembling as a dangerous instrument which might fail, and wound her in its recoil. But as days passed on, and each one brought him to the Cottage, or found Lucia with Mrs. Bellairs, and therefore in his society, it began to seem incredible that his coming was an event of only a few weeks ago; the past seemed to have receded, and this present, so

Mrs. Harry Coghill

bright and perfect, to be all her life. Yet, in truth, she had no notion of anatomizing her thoughts or feelings. They had come to be largely, almost wholly occupied by a new inmate, but she was simply content that it should be so, without once considering the subject.

One person, however, spent many bitter thoughts upon this recent change. To Maurice Leigh every day had brought a more thorough knowledge of Lucia's infatuation and of his own loss. He had loved her almost all his life, and would love her faithfully now, and always; but he began to be aware now, that he required more of her than the affection which he could still claim; that he wanted her daily companionship; her sympathy in all that interested him; her confidence with regard to all that concerned herself. He wanted all this; but he could do without it: he could love her and wait, if that were all. But what was hardest, nay, almost unendurable, was the anticipation of her day of disenchantment, when she must see the truth as he saw it now, and find herself thrown aside to learn, in solitude and suffering, how blindly she had suffered herself to be duped by a fair appearance. For, of course, Maurice was unjust. Seeing Lucia daily as she grew up, he had no idea how much the charm of her grace and beauty had influenced even him, and failed utterly to estimate their effect upon others. He said to himself that Mr. Percy was a mere selfish fop, who, tired of the amusements of Europe and too effeminate for the hardier enjoyments of a new country, was driven by mere emptiness of head to occupy himself with the pursuit of the prettiest woman he met with.

Meanwhile Mr. Percy came and went, and found in his visits to the Cottage an entirely new kind of distraction. It was strange to him to find himself welcomed and valued, genuinely, if shyly, for his own sake. He had known vulgar women, who had flattered him because he was the son of an earl; and prudent ones who gave him but a carefully measured civility, because he was a portionless younger son. Here he knew that both facts were absolutely nothing; and egotist as he was, this knowledge stirred most powerfully such depths as his nature possessed. In Lucia's presence he became almost as unworldly as herself; he gave himself up half willingly, half unconsciously to the enjoyment of feelings which no woman less thoroughly simple and natural could have awakened; but, it is true that when he left her he left also this strange region of sensations - he returned precisely to his former self.

The only person, perhaps, who did him strict and complete justice was Mrs. Costello. She, who had peculiar reasons for looking with unspeakable terror upon the suitors whom her child's beauty was certain to attract, had weighed each look, word, gesture - gleaned such knowledge as she could of his life, past and present, and judged him at last with an accuracy which her intense interest in the subject made almost perfect. Over this result she both rejoiced and lamented; but for the present the one idea most constantly and strongly present to her was that Lucia must pass by-and-by, only too soon, out of the sweet hopes and dreams of girlhood, into the deep shadow which continually rested upon her own heart. She knew how youth, which has never suffered, rebels with passionate struggles against its first sorrows. She lived over and over again in imagination her child's predestined trial.

But away from the unquiet household at the Cottage, there was beginning to be much gossip with regard to all these things, and many speculations of the usual kind as to the issue of Mr. Percy's undisguised admiration for the beauty of Cacouna. Bella Latour was questioned on all sides, and finding the general thirst for information a source of considerable amusement, she did not scruple to supply her friends with plenty of materials for their comments. From Maurice Leigh, no such satisfaction was to be obtained - the most inveterate news-seekers gained nothing from him.

A party of young people were collected one evening at Mrs. Scott's - a house about a mile from Cacouna, in the opposite direction to the Cottage. Lucia had been invited, but Maurice, who arrived late, had brought a hasty note from her, excusing herself on the plea of her mother's not being well. Little notice was taken at the time, for all knew that Mrs. Costello had been looking ill lately, and it was therefore probable enough that she might be too much indisposed for Lucia to leave her. But later in the evening, when they were tired with dancing, a group of girls began to chatter as they sat in a corner.

"I wonder what is the matter with Mrs. Costello," said one. "Lucia seems to me to go out very little lately."

"She is better employed at home," replied another.

"You should have brought Mr. Percy, Bella," said Magdalen Scott.

"You did not invite him; and beside, I think we are better off without him."

"Why? Don't you like him?"

"Tolerably well, but I am getting tired of him."

"Tired of him already?"

"I'm not like you, Magdalen; I could not be content to spend my life looking at one person."

Magdalen blushed a little, but answered rather sharply,

"You mean to be an old maid, I suppose, then?"

"I think I shall. At any rate, I should if I were to be always required to be looking at or thinking about a man when I had married him."

Mrs. Scott here called her daughter away, and May Anderson asked,

"Why are you always teasing Magdalen so, Bella? She does not like it, I am sure."

"She should not be so stupid. Magdalen thinks her whole business in life is to sit still and look pretty for her cousin Harry's benefit. I wish she would wake up."

"Harry is quite content seemingly. He told George that he thought her prettier than Lucia Costello."

"What idiots men are!" said Bella. "I don't believe they ever care about anything except a pretty face; and they have not even eyes to see that with."

"They seem to see it well enough in some cases. I do not know what there is in Lucia except her prettiness to attract them, and she never has any want of admirers. There's Maurice Leigh perfectly miserable about her this minute, and Mr. Percy, they say, continually running after her."

"My dear May, you need not trouble your head about Maurice Leigh; he is quite able to take care of himself, and would not be at all obliged to you for pitying him. As for Mr. Percy, the mere idea of his running anywhere or after anything!"

"Well, is not he perpetually at the Cottage?"

"He was not there yesterday."

"No, because Lucia was in Cacouna. I passed your house in the afternoon, and saw them both in the garden."

"They are both fond of flowers."

"I hear he goes to help her to garden."

"Mr. Percy help anybody!"

"To hinder, then; I dare say Lucia finds it equally amusing."

"Where is he this evening? Did he go with Mr. and Mrs. Bellairs?"

"No. And I was afraid I should have to stay at home and do the honours; but he had heard that I intended being here, and was polite enough to insist on my coming. He was out when I left."

"At the Cottage, of course. No wonder Lucia could not come."

While her friends thus charitably judged her, Lucia was, in truth, painfully and anxiously occupied by the illness of her mother. Mr. Percy, aware of her engagement for the evening, had ridden over early in the afternoon and spent an hour or two lounging beside her, at the piano or on the verandah. At last, when it grew nearly time for her to start for Mrs. Scott's, he rose to go.

"Come into the garden for a minute," he said. "It is growing cool now, and the air from the river is so pleasant."

She obeyed, and they wandered down the garden together. But the minute lengthened to twenty before they came back, and parted at the wicket. Lucia went slowly up the steps, disinclined to go in out of the sunshine, which suited her mood. Mrs. Costello had left her chair and her work on the verandah and gone indoors. Lucia picked up a fallen knitting-needle, and carried it into the parlour; but as she passed the doorway she saw her mother sitting in her own low chair, her head fallen forward, and her whole attitude strange and unnatural.

Lucia uttered a cry of terror; she sprang to Mrs. Costello's side, and tried to raise her, but the inanimate figure slipped from her arms. She called Margery, and together they lifted her mother and laid her on her bed. The first inexpressible fear soon passed away - it was but a deep fainting fit, which began to yield to their remedies. As soon as this became evident, Lucia had time to wonder what could have caused so sudden an illness. She remembered having seen a letter lying on the table beside her mother, and the moment she could safely leave the bedside she went in search of it. It was only an empty envelope, but as she moved away her dress rustled against a paper on the floor, which she picked up and found to be the letter itself. Without any other thought than that her mother must have received a shock which this might explain, she opened the half-folded sheet and hastily read the contents. They were short, and in a hand she knew well - that of a clergyman who was an old and trusted friend of Mrs. Costello. This was his letter: -

"My dear friend,

"I was just about writing to say that I would obey your summons, and steal two or three days next week from my work to visit you, when a piece of information reached me, which has caused me, for your sake, to defer my journey. Perhaps you can guess what it is. You have too often expressed your fears of C.'s return to be surprised at their fulfilment, but I grieve to have to add to your anxieties at this moment by telling you that he is really in this neighbourhood. I have not seen him, but one of my people, Mary Wanita, who remembers you affectionately, brought me the news. You may depend upon my guarding, with the utmost care, my knowledge of your retreat; but I thought it best to prepare you for the possibility of discovery, lest he should present himself unexpectedly to you or to Lucia. If the matter on which you wished to consult me is one that can be entrusted to a letter, write fully, and I will give you the best advice I can; but send your letter to the post-office at Claremont, on the American side, and I will myself call there for it. I shall also post my letters to you there for the present.

"With every good wish for you and for your child, believe me, sincerely yours,

"A. STRAFFORD."

Lucia had looked for a solution of the mystery, but this letter was none. Rather it was a new and bewildering problem. That it was the immediate cause of her mother's illness was evident enough, but why? Who was "C."? Why did she fear his return? What could be the fear strong enough to induce such precautions for secrecy? Her senses seemed utterly confused. But after the first few minutes, she remembered that Mrs. Costello had probably meant to keep her still ignorant of a mystery to which she had, in all the recollections of her life, no single clue - she might therefore be still further agitated by knowing that she had read this letter. "I must put it aside," she thought, "and not tell her until she is well again."

She slipped the letter into her pocket, scribbled her note to Mrs. Scott, and returned to the invalid's room. The faintness had now quite passed away, and Lucia thought, as she entered, that her mother's eyes turned to her with a peculiar look of inquiry. Happily the room was dark, so that the burning colour which rose to her cheeks was not perceptible; for the rest, she contrived to banish all consciousness from her voice, as she said quietly, "I have been writing to Mrs. Scott, to say I cannot leave you to-night."

"I am sorry, dear; you would have enjoyed yourself, and there is no reason to be anxious about me."

"I am very glad I was not gone. Can you go to sleep?"

"Presently. I think I dropped a letter - have you seen it?"

Lucia drew it from her pocket. "It is here, I picked it up."

Mrs. Costello held out her hand for it. She looked at it for a moment, as if hesitating - then slipped it under her pillow.

Both remained silent for some time; Mrs. Costello, exhausted and pale as death, lay trying to gather strength for thought and endurance, longing, yet dreading, to share with her daughter the miserable burden which was pressing out her very life. Lucia, half hidden by the curtain, sat pondering uselessly over the letter she had read; feeling a vague fear and a livelier curiosity. But a heart so ignorant of sadness in itself, and so filled at the moment with all that is least in accord with the prosaic troubles of middle life, could not remain long fixed upon a doubtful and uncomprehended misfortune. Gradually her fancy reverted to brighter images; the sunny life of her short experience, the only life she could believe in with a living faith, had its natural immutability in her thoughts; and she unconsciously turned from the picture which had been forced upon her - of her mother shrinking terrified from a calamity about to involve them both - to the brighter one of her own happiness which that dear mother could not help but share. So strangely apart were the two who were nearest to each other.

Mrs. Costello was the first to rouse herself.

"Light the lamp, dear," she said, "and let us have tea. I suppose I must not get up again."

"No indeed. I will bring my work in here and sit by you."

"Will Maurice be here to-night?"

"He is at the Scotts."

"True, I forgot. We shall be alone, then?"

It was a question; a month ago it would have been an assertion; and Lucia answered, "Yes."

"Then we may arrange ourselves here without fear of interruption," Mrs. Costello said more cheerfully. "Bring a book, instead of your work, and read to me."

She did not then intend to explain Mr. Strafford's letter. Lucia had almost hoped it, but on the other hand she feared, as perhaps her mother did, to renew the afternoon's excitement.

So, after tea, she took the last new book and read. Mrs. Costello lay with her face shaded; she had much to think of, -

only old debatings with herself to go over again for the thousandth time; but all her doubts, her wishes, her fears quickened into new life by the threatened discovery, of which the letter lying under her pillow had warned her; and the changes which a multitude of recollections brought to her countenance were not for her child, still ignorant of all the past, to see.

The evening passed quickly in this tumult of thoughts. Lucia was interested in her story, and read on until ten o'clock, when Margery came in.

"Mr. Maurice, Miss Lucia. He came in at the back, just to ask how your mamma is. Will you speak to him?"

Lucia went out. Maurice was standing in the dark parlour, and she almost ran against him. He put his hand lightly on her shoulder, as he asked his question.

"She is better, very much better," she answered. "But I was frightened at first."

"Do you think it is only a passing affair? Are you afraid to be alone to-night?"

"Not at all. Oh! Maurice, why do you ask such a question? She was quite well this morning."

"She has not looked well for some time. But I did not mean to alarm you, only to remind you that if you should want anything, I am always close at hand."

He had alarmed her a little for the moment. She thought, "I have been occupied with myself, and she has been ill perhaps for days past." Maurice felt her tremble, and blamed himself for speaking. At that instant they seemed to have returned to their old life. The very attitude in which they stood, in which they had been used to have their most confidential chats, had lately been disused; and to resume it, and with it the old position of adviser and consoler, was compensation for much that he had suffered. He felt that Lucia was looking anxiously up at him - that she had for the moment quite forgotten all except her mother and himself.

"The weather has been so hot," he said, searching for something to hide his thoughts, "it is not wonderful for any one to be weakened by it. No doubt, that was the reason of Mrs. Costello's illness." Lucia remembered the letter and was silent. Then she said, "Have you really thought her looking ill lately?"

"'Ill' is perhaps too strong a word. Besides, she has always said she was well."

"Yes. But I know she has been" - in trouble, she was going to say, but stopped - "suffering."

"Perhaps you may be able to nurse her a little now, since she will be obliged to own herself an invalid."

"I shall try. Will you come in for a moment, in the morning?"

"Yes. Good night now. Do not be too anxious."

He went out, glad at heart because of those few words of hers, which showed how naturally she still depended on him, when help of any kind was needed.

Mrs. Costello had lain, during his visit, listening to the faint sound of their voices, which just reached her through the half-open door of her room.

She turned her head restlessly as she listened. "If it could have been," she thought, "he would have been the same to her through all - but the other, how could I tell him even? Truly, I believe he would forgive crime, more readily than misery like mine. And I *must* tell her."

Lucia came back softly into the room, and to the bedside; looking, with her newly awakened fears, at her mother's face, she saw plainly how worn it was; it seemed, in truth, to have grown years older in the last few weeks. A pang of remorse shot through her heart; she stooped and kissed her with unusual tenderness, and then turned away to hide the tears which self-reproach had brought to her eyes. Mrs. Costello caught her hand, and smiling, asked what news Maurice had brought?

"None, mamma. He came to ask about you."

"But had he nothing to tell you about the Scotts?"

"I forgot to ask him, and I believe he forgot to tell me."

"You must have been very much interested to forget such an event as a party the moment it was over."

"We were only talking about you. Maurice says you have been looking ill."

"Maurice is a foolish boy. I have been a little worried, but that is all."

Lucia gathered all her courage. "But, dear mother, why do you always give me that answer? Why not tell me what it is that troubles you?"

Mrs. Costello shrank back. "Not yet, darling. I am a coward, and should have to tell you a long story. Wait awhile."

"And while I wait, you suffer alone."

"I should not suffer less, my child, if you knew all. For your own sake I have not yet shared my troubles, such as they are, with you; for your own sake I see that I must soon do so. Leave me at present to decide, if I can, what is best for us both."

Lucia was silent. She saw that even this short conversation had disturbed, instead of comforting her mother; she dared not therefore say more, and could only busy herself in arranging everything with affectionate care for her comfort during the night.

Next morning when Maurice came, he was surprised to find Mrs. Costello up, and looking as usual. Lucia's uneasiness had almost melted away in the daylight; she was more gentle and attentive than usual to her mother, but had persuaded herself that with her care, and, above all, with her sympathy, when the promised "long story" should be told, all would come right. She had still, however, enough need of sympathy to make her manner to Maurice such as he liked best. He went away a second time very happy, thinking, "She is but a child. If that fellow were but gone she would soon forget him, and be herself again."

But, alas! "that fellow" showed no intention of going. He came to the Cottage an hour or two later, not however alone, but with Mrs. Bellairs and Bella. The former came to see Mrs. Costello, the latter had affairs of her own with Lucia. Mr. Percy, for once, was decidedly *de trop*, but after awhile the two girls slipped away and shut themselves up in Lucia's bedroom. The moment the door was closed, Bella burst into a torrent of talk.

"Oh! my dear, I was determined to come to you this morning, but I dare say it was trouble thrown away. Have you any attention to spare from your own affairs for your neighbours?"

"Plenty. How did you enjoy yourself last night?"

"You shall hear. It was a dull enough evening till the very end. There was Maurice looking as black as thunder at May Anderson; and Magdalen Scott and Harry - not flirting, they have not sense enough for that - but making themselves ridiculous; and everybody else as usual."

"Why was Maurice looking black at May?"

Mrs. Harry Coghill

"Because she was talking about you. It's not safe for anybody to talk about you before Maurice, I can tell you. But *I* don't want to talk about them, but about myself. Do you know what has happened?"

"How should I till you tell me?"

"Well, you might guess; but, I suppose, since Mr. Percy came, he has prevented you from seeing anything beyond himself."

"Don't be absurd, Bella; I can always see you, at any rate."

"And yet you can't guess? Well, then, my dear, I have altered my mind."

"What about?"

"Only yesterday I meant to be an old maid, and now I don't."

Lucia clapped her hands. "Oh, Bella! is it Doctor Morton?"

"I suppose so. You see it would be more convenient for me in some ways to be married; Elise and William might get tired of too much of my society, and no doubt it will suit him very well to have a house rent-free and a little money besides."

"Don't, Bella, you are incorrigible. I should think you might leave off joking now."

"Not I, I assure you. I leave the sentimental side of the question to you and Mr. Percy; though, to tell you the truth, I think you would be much better off in that respect with Maurice, and his highflown notions, which Elise calls chivalrous."

Certainly Bella's manner agreed with her words - never was so important a piece of news told by one girl to another, in so calm and business-like a style. Lucia, rather given to romance herself, was puzzled and half shocked.

When the visitors were gone, she repeated what she had heard to her mother, with wondering comments on a compact so coolly arranged, and was rather surprised to find that Mrs. Costello completely approved of it.

"I dare say," she said, "it may be a very happy marriage. Doctor Morton is a sensible man, and Bella too honest a girl to marry him if she did not mean to behave as he would like her."

And this, then, was her mother's idea of a happy marriage. Lucia wondered still more, yet less than she would have done if she had known how gladly Mrs. Costello would have seen her, also, safely bestowed in the keeping of "a sensible man."

Mrs. Harry Coghill

CHAPTER V

At the time when Bella informed Lucia of her engagement, her newly-accepted lover was having a long conversation with her brother-in-law and guardian. There was no reason why the marriage once arranged should be delayed; on the contrary, everybody was happily agreed in the opinion that it might take place almost immediately. The conference of the two gentlemen, therefore, passed readily into the region of business, and chiefly concerned dollars and cents.

Mr. Latour, the father of Mrs. Bellairs and Bella, had died rich; all his property in hind, houses, and money was carefully divided between the sisters; and as he had been dead less than two years, very slight changes had taken place during Mr. Bellairs' guardianship. Bella spoke reasonably enough when she said her fortune would be acceptable to Doctor Morton. He made no secret of the fact that it would be very acceptable, and Mr. Bellairs - though, for his own part, he would have married his charming Elise with exactly the same eagerness if she had been penniless - was too sensible to be at all displeased with his future brother-in-law's clear and straightforward manner of treating so important a subject. It is true that his brains and his diploma were almost all the capital the young man had to bring on his side, but these, had their acknowledged value, and, after all, Bella was very nearly of age, and it would be rather a comfort to see her safely disposed of, instead of having to give up her guardianship into her own giddy keeping.

Mr. Bellairs' office was a small wooden-frame building

containing two rooms. In the outer one half-a-dozen budding lawyers, in various stages, sat at their desks; the inner one, where the two gentlemen discussed their arrangements, was small, and contained only a stove, a writing-table, two chairs, and some cupboards. Mr. Bellairs sat at the table with a pile of papers before him: in the second chair - an easy one - Doctor Morton lounged, and amused himself while he talked, by tracing the pattern of the empty stove with the end of a small cane. He was a good-looking young man, with very black eyes, and a small black beard; of middle height and strongly built, and noted in Cacouna as the boldest rider, the best swimmer, and one of the best shots, in the neighbourhood.

A little stir, and a loud rough voice speaking in the outer office, was followed by the entrance of a clerk.

"Here is Clarkson, sir. Says he must see you."

A shaggy head appeared over the clerk's shoulder, and the same rough voice called out, "Just a minute, Mr. Bellairs; it's only a small matter of business."

Mr. Bellairs went out, drawing the door together after him, and after a few minutes dismissed the man, and came back.

"That fellow may give you some trouble," he said as he sat down again.

"Me? How?" asked the Doctor, surprised.

"Some years ago, Mr. Latour bought a hundred acres of wild land on Beaver Creek. He took no trouble about it, except what he was actually obliged; never even saw it, I believe; and about a year before his death, this Clarkson squatted on it, built a house, married, and took his wife to live there. Mr. Latour heard of all this by chance, and went to see if it were true. There, he found the fellow comfortably settled, and expecting nothing less than to be turned out. The end of the matter, for that time, was, that Clarkson promised to pay some

Mrs. Harry Coghill

few dollars rent, and was left in possession. The rent, however, never was paid. Mr. Latour died, and when his affairs came into my hands I tried again to get it; threatened to turn Clarkson out, and pull down his house if he did not pay, and certainly would have done it, but for Bella, to whom I should tell you the land belongs. Mrs. Clarkson came into town, and went to her with such a pitiful story that she persuaded me to wait. The consequence is that nothing has been done yet, though I believe it is altogether misplaced kindness to listen to their excuses."

"I have no doubt it is."

"Clarkson is a great scamp, but I hear his wife is a very decent woman, and naturally Bella was humbugged."

"Naturally, yes. But I hope it is not too late to get rid of such tenants, or make them pay?"

"I would rather you undertook the task than I, except, of course, in the way of business. Professionally, a lawyer has no tenderness for people who can't pay."

"And in what condition is the rest of the land?"

"Much as it always was. The Indians are the only people who profit by it at present; they hunt over it, and dry the fish they catch in the creek, along the bank."

"Yet, if it were cleared, it ought not to be a bad position. Where is it on the creek?"

Mr. Bellairs reached a map, and the two became absorbed in discussing the probable advantages of turning out Clarkson and the Indians, and clearing the farm on Beaver Creek.

Mr. Bellairs left his office earlier than usual that day, and found his wife sitting alone in her little morning room. He took up a magazine which lay on the table, and seated himself comfortably in an easy-chair opposite to her.

"Where's Bella?" he asked presently.

"Upstairs, I believe. She and I have nearly quarrelled to-day."

"What about?"

"About her marriage. I declare, William, I have no patience with her."

Mr. Bellairs laughed. "An old complaint, my dear; but why?"

"She is so matter-of-fact. I asked her, at last, what she was going to marry for, and she told me coolly, for convenience."

Mrs. Bellairs' indignation made her husband laugh still more. "They are well matched," he said; "Morton is as cool as she is. He might be Bluebeard proposing for his thirteenth wife."

"Well, *you* may like it, but I don't. If they care so little about eachother now, what will they do when they have been married as long as we have?"

"My dear Elise, you and I were born too soon. *We* never thought of marrying for convenience; but as our ideas on the subject don't seem to have changed much in ten years, perhaps theirs may not do so either. By the way, where's Percy?"

"That's another thing. I don't want to be inhospitable to your cousin, but I do wish with all my heart that he was back in England."

Mr. Bellairs threw his magazine on the table. "Why, what on earth is the matter with him?"

"Do you know where he spends half his time?"

"Not I. To tell the truth, his listless, dawdling way rather

　　　　　Mrs. Harry Coghill

provokes me, and I have not been sorry to see less of him lately."

"He goes to the Cottage every day."

"Does he? I should not have thought that an amusement much in his way."

"You say yourself that Lucia is a wonderfully pretty girl."

"Lucia? She is a child. You don't think that attracts him?"

Mrs. Bellairs was silent.

"Elise, don't be absurd. You women are always fancying things of that kind. A fellow like Percy is not so easily caught."

"I hope to goodness I am only fancying, but I believe you would give Mrs. Costello credit for some sense, and she is certainly uneasy."

"Does she say so?"

"No. But I know it; and Maurice and Lucia are not the same friends they used to be."

"Lucia must be an idiot if she can prefer Percy to Maurice; but most girls do seem to be idiots."

"In the meantime, what to do? I feel as if we were to blame."

"We can't very well turn out my honourable cousin. I suspect the best thing to do is to leave them alone. *He* will not forget to take care of himself."

"He? No fear. But it is of her I think. I should be sorry to see her married to him, even if the Earl would consent."

"It will never come to that. And, after all, you may be mistaken in supposing there is anything more than a little flirtation."

Mrs. Bellairs shook her head, but said no more. She knew by experience that her husband would remember what he had heard, and take pains to satisfy himself as to the cause of her anxiety. She had also (after ten years of wedlock!) implicit faith in his power to do something, she did not know what, to remedy whatever was wrong.

That evening, when the whole family were assembled, the half-abandoned scheme of passing a long day in the country was revived, and the time finally settled. It was agreed that Doctor Morton, Lucia, and Maurice should be the only persons invited; but when all the other arrangements had been made, it appeared that Maurice had some particularly obstinate engagement which refused to be put off, and he was, therefore, of necessity left behind.

The morning fixed for the excursion proved breathlessly hot; the sky was of one unvaried, dazzling, blue, and the waters of the river seemed to rise above their banks, while every object, even houses and trees at a considerable distance, was reflected in them with a clearness which foretold stormy weather. A note from Mrs. Bellairs had prepared Lucia, and she was standing on the verandah, dangling her hat in her hand, when Mr. and Mrs. Bellairs drove up. She only stopped to give her mother a last hasty kiss, and then ran out to meet them.

The others had gone on, and were dawdling along the road, when Bob, at his usual sober trot, turned out of the lane - Doctor Morton driving with Bella, Mr. Percy on horseback. The party moved on leisurely, too hot to think of a quicker movement, and, as was natural, Mr. Percy drew his horse to the side of the phaeton where Lucia sat. A drive of three miles brought them to the farm, where they left the horses in the care of a servant, and walked across a wide, unenclosed space of green to the house. It was a long, ugly building, with innumerable windows. The walls were whitewashed, and glared out painfully in the sunshine; the roof, window-frames, and doors painted a dull red; but the situation, similar to that of Mrs. Costello's Cottage, was lovely, and a group of fine trees standing just where the green bank began to slope down abruptly to the river, gave a delicious shade to that side of the building and to some seats placed under them. Mr. Latour, in letting the house, had retained one room for his daughters, who were fond of the place, and they still kept possession of it. Here they were to dine; for the rest of the day, out of doors was much pleasanter than in.

A boat and fishing-tackle were at hand, but it was too hot to fish; after wandering about a little, they all sat down under the trees. Mrs. Bellairs, Bella, and Lucia had some pretence of work in their hands; the three gentlemen lounged on the grass near them. The farmer's children, at play at the end of the house, occasionally darted out to peep at them, and flew back again the moment they were perceived. Everything else was still, even the leaves overhead did not move, and the silence was so infectious that by degrees all talk ceased - each had his or her own dreams for the moment. Bella and Doctor Morton, utterly unromantic pair of lovers as they were, must have had some touch of the ordinary softness of human nature; they looked content with all the world. Lucia, leaning back with her crochet lying on her lap, and her eyes half hidden by their black lashes, had yielded herself up entirely to the indolent enjoyment of perfect stillness, forgetting even to be conscious of the pair of handsome blue eyes which rested on her, taking in luxuriously the charm of her beauty.

When this pause had lasted a minute or two, a sudden glance passed between Mr. and Mrs. Bellairs. His said, "I am afraid you were right;" - hers, "What shall we do?" to which he replied by getting up, and saying,

"Are you all going to sleep, good people?"

A reluctant stir, and change of position among the group, answered him.

"What else can we do?" asked Bella. "It is too hot to move."

"If you intend to go on the river to-day, it had better be soon," said her brother-in-law. "There is every appearance of a storm coming on."

"Not before we get home, I hope. But look, there is a canoe."

As she spoke, a small object came darting across the river. It approached so fast, that in a minute or two they could distinguish plainly that it was, in fact, a tiny bark canoe. One Indian woman, seated at the end, seemed to be its only occupant; the repeated flashes of sunlight on her paddle showed how quick and dexterous were its movements as she steered straight for the landing in front of the farmhouse.

"Look here, Percy," said Mr. Bellairs; "I don't believe you have seen a squaw yet. Get up and quote appropriate poetry on the occasion."

"'Hiawatha' I suppose? I don't know any," and Mr. Percy rose lazily. "She is an odd figure. How do you know it's a woman at all?"

"Don't you see the papoose lying in the canoe?"

"Conclusive evidence, certainly; but upon my word the lady's costume is not particularly feminine."

They were all standing up now, watching the canoe which had drawn quite near the bank. In a minute or two longer it touched the land, and the woman rose. She was of small size, but rather squarely built; her long jet black hair, without ornament or attempt at dressing, hung loosely down over her shoulders; she wore mocassins of soft yellow leather ornamented with beads; trousers of black cloth, with a border of the same kind of work, reached her ankles; a cloth skirt, almost without fulness, came a little below the knee, and was covered, to within three or four inches of its edge, by an equally scanty one of red and white cotton, with a kind of loose bodice and sleeves, attached to it; a blanket, fastened round her shoulders in such a manner that it could be drawn over her head like a monk's cowl, completed her dress. A little brown baby, tightly swathed in an old shawl, lay at her feet, exposed, seemingly without discomfort, to the hot glare of the sun. She stood a moment, as if examining the house, and the group of figures in front of it; then picked up her child, slipped it into the folds of her blanket, so that it hung safely on her back, its black eyes peeping out over her shoulders, took a bundle of mats from under the seat of her canoe, and stepped on shore.

As she came, with light firm steps, up the bank, not exactly approaching them, but turning to the house-door, the party under the trees separated; the gentlemen, attracted by the lightness and beauty of the canoe, went down to the water's edge to look at it more closely. Bella wanted to see the papoose, and perhaps to bargain with its mother for some of her work; Mrs. Bellairs and Lucia remained alone, when the former, turning to say something to her companion, was surprised to see her pale, trembling, and looking ready to faint.

"My dear child," she cried in alarm, "what is the matter, you are ill?"

"Not ill, only stupid. Don't mind me. I shall be quite right again in a minute." But her breath came in gasps, and her very lips were white.

"Will you come in? Can you walk?"

"No, no; it is nothing." By a strong effort she recovered herself a little, and smiled. "Could anything be so absurd?"

"What was it? I can't understand."

"That poor woman. Is not it strange the sight of an Indian or a squaw always throws me into a kind of panic. I am horribly frightened, and I don't know why."

"It is strange, certainly; what are you afraid of?"

"Of nothing at all. I cannot think why I should feel so, but I always have. Indeed I try not to be so foolish."

"I can't scold you for it at present, for you really frightened me, and you are generally fearless enough."

"I am so glad there was no one but you here. Please do not tell anybody."

"But do you know, child, that you are still as pale as ever you can be? And they are coming back from the river. Your enemy is out of sight now; let us walk up to the house."

They put on their hats, and walked slowly up the sunny slope; but as they came upon the level space in front of the house, the squaw, who had been bargaining with the farmer's wife at a side door, came round the corner and met them face to face. She paused a moment, and then walked straight up to the two ladies, holding out her mats as an invitation to them to buy. Lucia shrank back, and Mrs. Bellairs afraid, from her previous alarm, that she really would faint, motioned hastily to the woman to go away. But she seemed in no hurry to obey; repeating in a monotonous tone, "Buy, buy," she stood still, fixing her eyes upon Lucia with a keen look of inquiry. The poor child, terrified, and ashamed of being so, made an uncertain movement towards the door, when the squaw suddenly laid her hand upon her arm.

"Where live?" she said, in broken English.

"Go, go!" cried Mrs. Bellairs impatiently. "We have nothing for you;" and taking Lucia's arm, she drew her into their sitting-room, and shut the door.

"Lie down on the sofa;" she said, "what could the woman

mean? You must have an opposite effect on her to what she has on you. But you need not fear any more; she is going down to her canoe."

By degrees, Lucia's panic subsided, her colour came back, and she regained courage to go out and meet the others. They found that Doctor Morton and Bella had strolled away along the shore, while the other two were occupied in discussing Indian customs and modes of life, their conversation having started from the bark canoe. The two ladies took their work, and remained quiet listeners, until a rough-looking, untidy servant-girl came to tell them dinner was ready.

Fish caught that morning, and fowls killed since the arrival of the party, were on the table; the untidy servant had been commissioned by her mistress to wait, which she did by sitting down and looking on with great interest while dinner proceeded. It was not a particularly satisfactory meal in its earlier stages, but all deficiencies were atoned for by the appearance of a huge dish of delicious wild raspberries, and a large jug of cream, which formed the second course.

As soon as dinner was over, the boat was brought out, and they spent an hour or two on the river; but the weather had already begun to change, and, to avoid the approaching storm, they were obliged to leave the farm much earlier than they had intended, and hasten towards home. When they approached the Cottage, Lucia begged to be set down, that her friends might not be hindered by turning out of their way to take her quite home; Mr. Bellairs drew up, therefore, at the end of the lane, and Lucia sprang out. Mr. Percy, however, insisted on going with her. He dismounted and led his horse beside her.

"I am sure you will be wet," she said; "you forget that I am a Canadian girl, and quite used to running about by myself."

"That may be very well," he answered, "when you have no one at your disposal for an escort, but at present the case is different."

She blushed a little and smiled. "In England would people be shocked at my going wherever I please alone?"

"I don't know; I believe I am forgetting England and everything about it. Do you know that I ought to be there now?"

"Ought? that is a very serious word. But you are not going yet?"

"Not just yet. Miss Costello, your mother is an Englishwoman, why don't you persuade her to bring you to England."

"My mother will never go to England." Lucia repeated the words slowly like a lesson learned by rote; and as she did so, an old question rose again in her mind, - why not?

"Yet you long to go - you have told me so."

"Yes, oh! I do long to go. It seems to me like Fairyland."

It was Mr. Percy's turn to smile now. "Not much like Fairyland," he answered; "not half so much like it as your own Canada."

"Well, perhaps I shall see it some day, but then alone. Without mamma, I should not care half so much."

"Are you still so much a child? 'Without mamma' would be no great deprivation to most young ladies."

"I cannot understand that. But then we have always been together; we could hardly live apart."

"Not even if you had - Doctor Morton for instance, to take care of you?"

Lucia laughed heartily at the idea, and Mr. Percy laughed too, though his sentence had begun seriously enough. They were

Mrs. Harry Coghill

now at the gate, he bade her good-bye, and springing on his horse, went away at a pace which was meant to carry off a considerable amount of irritation against himself. "I had nearly made a pretty fool of myself," he soliloquised. "It is quite time I went away from here. But what a sweet little piece of innocence she is, and so lovely! I do not believe anything more perfect ever was created. Pshaw! who would have thought of *my* turning sentimental?"

As Lucia turned from the gate, Margery put her head round the corner of the house, and beckoned.

"Your ma's lying down, Miss Lucia, - at least I guess so, - and she doesn't expect you yet, and I've something to tell you."

Lucia went into the kitchen and sat down. She was feeling tired after the heat of the day, and the excitement of her alarm, and expected only to hear some tale of household matters. But to her surprise Margery began, "There've been a squaw here to-day, and, you know, they don't come much about Cacouna, thank goodness, nasty brown things - but this one, she came with her mats and rubbish, in a canoe, to be sure. Your ma, she was out, and I caught sight of something coming up the bank towards the house, so I went out on the verandah to see. As soon as she saw me, she held up her mats and says, 'Buy, buy, buy,' making believe she knew no more English than that, but I told her we wanted none of her goods, and then she said, 'Missis at home?' I told her no, and she said 'Where?' as impudent as possible. I told her that was none of her business, and she'd better go; but instead of that, she took hold of my gown, and she said "Lucia" as plain as possible. I do declare, Miss Lucia, I did not know what to make of her, for how she should come to know your name was queer anyhow; but I just said, Mrs. Costello is not in, nor Miss Lucia neither, so you'd better be off; and she nodded her head a lot of times, and seemed as if she were considering whether to go or not. I asked her what she wanted, but she would not tell me, and after awhile she went off again in her canoe as fast as if she was going express."

Lucia was thoroughly startled by this story. Mr. Strafford's letter came to her mind, and connected itself with the singular look and manner of the squaw, at the farm. This could not certainly be the mysterious "C." of the letter, for Mr. Strafford said "*he* is in the neighbourhood," but it might be Mary Wanita, who had apparently given the first friendly warning, and might possibly have come to Cacouna for the purpose of giving a second, and more urgent one.

"Where was mamma?" she asked.

"Gone in to see Mr. Leigh," Margery answered; "he is quite sick to-day, and Mr. Maurice came to ask your mamma to go and sit with him awhile."

"Did you tell her about this squaw?"

"Well, no, Miss Lucia, I had a kind of guess it was better not. You see she is not very strong, and I thought you could tell her when you came if you thought it was any use."

"Thank you, Margery, you were quite right."

Lucia went in slowly, thinking the matter over. It did not, however, appear to her advisable to conceal from her mother the squaw's visit - it might have greater significance than she, knowing so little, could imagine - but she wished extremely that she possessed some gauge by which to measure beforehand the degree of agitation her news was likely to produce. She had none, however, and could devise no better plan than that of telling Mrs. Costello, quite simply, what she had just heard from Margery.

As she opened the door of the parlour, Mrs. Costello half rose from the sofa, where she was lying.

"Is it you, darling," she asked, "so soon?"

"There is a storm coming on," Lucia answered; "we hurried

home to escape it."

"And you have had a pleasant day?"

"Very pleasant. You have been out, too?"

"Yes; poor Mr. Leigh is quite an invalid, and complains that he never sees you now."

"I will go to-morrow," Lucia said hastily, and then, glad to escape from the subject, asked if her mother had seen an Indian woman about?

Mrs. Costello answered no, but Lucia felt her start, and went on to repeat, in as unconcerned a tone as possible, Margery's story; but when she said that her own name had been mentioned, her mother stopped her.

"Was the woman a stranger? Have you ever seen her?"

"She was a stranger to Margery certainly. I think I saw her to-day."

"Where? Tell me all you know of her."

Lucia described the squaw's appearance at the farm.

"It must be Mary," Mrs. Costello said half to herself. "What shall I do? How escape?"

She rose from the sofa and walked with hurried steps up and down the room. Lucia watched her in miserable perplexity till she suddenly stopped.

"Is that all?" she asked. "Did she go away?"

Lucia finished her account, and when she had done so, Mrs. Costello came back to the sofa and sat down. She put her arm round her daughter, and drawing her close to her, she said,

"You are a good child, Lucia, for you ask no questions, though you may well think your mother ought to trust you. Be patient only a little longer, till I have thought all over. Perhaps we shall be obliged to go away. I cannot tell."

"Away from Cacouna, mamma?"

"Away from Cacouna and from Canada. Away from all you love - can you bear it?"

"Yes - with you;" but the first pang of parting came with those words.

CHAPTER VI

"Away from all you love!" The words haunted Lucia after she lay down in her little white bed that night. There, in the midst of every object familiar to her through all her life, surrounded by the perfect atmosphere of home, she repeated, with wondering trouble, the threat that had come to her. When at last she slept, these words, and the pale face of her mother bending over her as she closed her eyes, mixed themselves with her dreams. At last, she fancied that a violent storm had come on in the very noon of a brilliant summer day. She herself, her mother, Percy and Maurice seemed to be standing on the river bank watching how the sky darkened, and the water rose in great waves at their feet. Suddenly a canoe appeared, and in it a hideous old squaw, who approached the shore, and stretching out a long bony hand drew her away from her mother's side, and in spite of her terror made her step into the frail boat, which instantly flew down the stream into the darkest and wildest of the storm. She stretched out her arms for help - Percy stood still upon the bank, as if anxious but unable to give it - Maurice waved his hand to her, and turned away. She seemed to know that he was deserting her for ever, and in an agony of fear and sorrow she gathered all her strength to call him back. The effort woke her. She lay trembling, with tears of agitation pouring from her eyes, while the storm which had mingled with her dream raged furiously round the Cottage.

Morning came at last, dim and dreary. The wind subsided at dawn, but the sky was full of torn and jagged clouds, carried hither and thither by its varying currents. All over the ground lay broken flowers and sprays torn from the trees, the vine had been loosened in several places from its fastenings and hung disconsolately over the verandah - all looked ravaged and desolate, as Lucia pressed her hot cheek against the rain-covered window, and tried to shake off the misery - still new to her - which belongs to the early morning after a restless, fevered night. But as the sun rose bright and warm, her spirits naturally revived; she dressed early, and went out into the garden, intent upon remedying as far as possible the mischief that had been done, before her mother should see it; and accustomed as she was to work among her much-beloved plants, the task was soon making quick progress. But among her roses, the most valued of all her flowers, a new discouragement awaited her. One beautiful tree, the finest of all, which yesterday had been splendid in the glory of its late blossoms, had been torn up by the wind, and flung down battered and half covered with sand at a little distance from the bed where it had grown. The sight of this misfortune seemed to Lucia almost more than she could bear; she sat down upon a garden-seat close by, and looked at her poor rose-tree as if its fate were to be a type of her own. She recollected a thousand trifles connected with it; how she had disputed with Mr. Percy about its beauty, arguing that it was less perfect than some others, because he had said it was more so; she remembered how from that very tree she had gathered a blossom for him the first day he came to the Cottage. Then, in her fanciful mood, she reproached herself for letting her unfortunate favourite speak to her only of him, and forgetting that it was Maurice who had obtained it for her, who had planted it, and would be sorry for its destruction. She rose, and tried to lift the broken tree; but as she leaned over it, Maurice himself passed through the wicket, and came towards her. She turned to meet him as if it were quite natural that he should come just then.

"Oh, Maurice, look! I am so sorry."

"Your pet rose-tree? But perhaps it will recover yet."

He raised it carefully, while she stood looking on.

"It is not much broken, after all. I will plant it again; and with plenty of support and shade, I think it will do."

Lucia flew to bring her spade. She held the tree, while Maurice carefully arranged its roots and piled the earth about them; the scattered leaves were picked up from the bed, and a kind of tent made with matting over the invalid; at last she found time to say,

"But how did you happen to come just at the right moment?"

"I saw you from my window. I noticed that you were very busy for awhile, and when you stopped working and sat down in that disconsolate attitude, I guessed some terrible misfortune must have happened. So I came."

Lucia looked at him gravely, a little troubled.

"I never saw anybody like you," she said; "you seem always to know when one is in a dilemma."

Maurice laughed.

"If all dilemmas were like this, I might easily get up a character for being a sort of Providence; but come and show me what else there is to do."

They worked together for an hour, by the end of which, all was restored nearly to its former neatness. Mrs. Costello came out and found them busy at the vine. Maurice was on a ladder nailing it up, while Lucia handed him the nails and strips of cloth, as he wanted them. She felt a lively pleasure in seeing them thus occupied. Maurice was too dear to her, for her not to have seen how Lucia's recent and gradual estrangement had troubled him; for his sake, therefore, as well as for her own and her child's, she had grieved daily over what she dared not interfere to prevent, - the breaking up of old habits, and the intervention between these two of an influence she dreaded. The experience of her own life had convinced her, rightly or wrongly, that it was worse than useless for parents to try to control their children's inclinations in the most important point where inclination ever ought to be made the rule of conduct. But for years she had hoped that Lucia's affection for Maurice would grow, unchecked and untroubled, till it attained that perfection which she thought the beau ideal of married love; and even now, she held tenaciously to such fragments of her old hope as still remained. This morning, after a night of the most painful anxiety and foreboding, her mind naturally caught at the idea that *all* could not go wrong with her; that she must have exaggerated the change in Lucia, and that, at least, some of the trouble she had anticipated for her child was a mere chimera.

She came out to them, therefore, pale and weary from her vigil, but cheerful and composed.

"How is your father, Maurice?" she asked; "can you stay with us to breakfast?"

"Thank you, no; my father is so much alone. He seemed better last night. Your visit did him good."

"I am glad of that. Lucia will go over to-day and stay with him for a while."

"Will she? He says she never comes to see him now."

"Indeed, I will," said Lucia, with a little remorse in her tone. "I will go and read the newspaper straight through to him, from one end to the other."

"Poor Lucia! What a sacrifice to friendship," answered Maurice laughing. "But to reward you, Blackwood arrived last night, and you will find the new chapter of your favourite story."

Soon after ten o'clock Lucia put on her hat, and, strong in her good resolutions, went along the lane to Mr. Leigh's. She lifted the latch rather timidly, and peeped in. From the tiny entrance she could see into the large square sitting-room, so tidy and so bare, from which the last trace of feminine occupation had passed away three years ago, when Alice Leigh, her old playfellow, died. There, in his high-backed chair, sat the solitary old man, prematurely old, worn out by labour and sorrow before his time. He turned his head at the sound of her entrance, and held out his hand, with a smile of welcome.

"My child, what a stranger you have grown!"

She came forward with a tender thrill of pity and affection.

"And you have been ill?" she said; "why did not you tell Maurice you wanted me?"

"Never mind, now. There is your own chair; sit down and tell me all your news."

She brought her chair to his side, and began to talk to him. How many happy hours she had spent in this room! Long ago, when she could first remember, when her mother and Mrs. Leigh had been dear friends; later, when there were yet others left of the ever-diminishing circle; later still, when Alice and Maurice were her daily companions; and even since, when she herself seemed to be, in the quiet household, the only representative of the daughters and sisters passed away. She felt that she had been selfish lately, and began to reproach herself the more strongly as she saw how affectionately she was still welcomed.

She told all the little scraps of news she could think of; she arranged on the mantelpiece some flowers she had brought in; finally, she found the new Blackwood, and entertained both her old friend and herself so well with it that two hours passed almost unperceived. Mr. Leigh's old servant, coming in with his early dinner, interrupted them in the middle of an interesting article, and reminded her that it was high time to go home.

"I will come again to-morrow," she said, as she put aside her book, and taking up her hat she hurried away.

As she walked up the lane, she could not help feeling a certain anxiety to know whether there had been any visitors at home during her absence. Mr. Percy often came in the morning, and if he had been there -

She ran up the verandah steps and into the parlour. Mrs. Costello sat there alone, and two letters lay on the table.

"Here is a note for you," she said, as Lucia came in. "Mr. Percy brought it."

"He has been here, then?" and she took up the note, not much caring to open it when she saw Bella's writing.

"Yes. He came very soon after you were gone. He said he was coming to say good-bye, and Bella asked him to bring that."

"To say good-bye?"

Lucia felt the colour fade out of her cheeks. She held the note in a tight grasp to keep her hand from trembling, and sat down.

"He and Mr. Bellairs are going up the Lakes. They will be back, I imagine, in a week or two. Perhaps, Bella tells you more."

In fact, Mr. Percy had been annoyed at not finding Lucia, and slightly discontented at being drawn into an excursion which would take him away from Cacouna. Only a small time yet remained before he *must* return to England, and he had been sufficiently conscious that Mrs. Costello would not regret his departure, to be very uncommunicative on the subject. Bella, however, was much more explicit.

"My dear Lucia," she said, " shall you be much surprised to

hear that these good people have arranged for a certain wedding, in which both you and I are interested, to take place on the first of next month; that is, not quite three weeks from to-day? How I am to be ready I do not know; but as you are to be bridesmaid, I implore you to come to me either this evening or to-morrow, that we may arrange about the dresses and so on. Is not it a mercy? William has taken into his head that he is obliged to go up the Lakes to Sault Ste. Marie, in the interest of some client or other, and has persuaded his cousin to go with him, so that Elise and I will be left in peace for our last few weeks together. They are to be back about the 26th, and I have done all I could to make Doctor Morton go with them, but he says if he does, the house will not be ready, so, I suppose, he must stay. They start by this evening's boat, and as the dearly beloved cousin is sure to go to see you first, I shall ask him to take my note. Entre nous, I don't believe he is particularly anxious to go. And you? I expect every time I come near the Cottage, I shall hear you singing your mother's favourite song:

> 'Alas! I scarce can go or creep,
> Now Lubin is away.'

Lubin! What a name! Mind you come, whatever else you do. Think of the importance of the subject. Dresses, my dear, wedding-dresses!

> "Ever yours,
> "BELLA."

Lucia read Bella's effusion hastily through, and gave it to her mother. Mrs. Costello laughed as she finished it.

"When will you go on this important errand?" she asked.

"Oh! not to-day, mamma, I am tired, and they don't really want me. I shall stay with you this afternoon."

"I have been writing to Mr. Strafford," Mrs. Costello said after a pause. "Some time ago I asked him to come up and see us; he could not do so then, but I hope now to be able to persuade him. I think, too, that the squaw who was here yesterday may be one of his people. Formerly I knew something of many of them; that might account for her coming. I have told him of it, and will do nothing until I receive his answer."

Lucia was silent; she longed to say something, but the conviction that her mother was quite decided in her reticence on the subject of the mystery, which was clearly so painful a one, restrained her. They dined, and spent the afternoon together without any further allusion to the subject; and Lucia was thankful to perceive that her mother's tranquillity seemed to have been far less disturbed by this second alarm than it had been by the first.

In the evening, quite late, Maurice came in. He said his father was much better. Lucia's long visit had cheered him and done him good, and he hoped in a day or two to be able to get out a little. Lucia was very quiet during Maurice's stay; it would not have been easy to say whether she was happy or sorrowful. She sat in her low chair and thought of yesterday, of the night and her dream, of old Mr. Leigh sitting alone in his dreary house so many hours each day, of his pleasure at seeing her, of Mr. Percy's absence; finally, of the comfort and pleasantness of sitting there undisturbed and hearing the voices of her mother and Maurice gradually subsiding into a drowsy hum. The next thing she knew Maurice was saying softly, "She is asleep. Don't wake her, Mrs. Costello. Good-night." And she woke just in time to catch the last glimpse of his figure as he went out.

The next day's consultation with Bella about dresses was only the first of many, in which the arrangements for the wedding were completely settled. Lucia and Magdalen Scott were to be bridesmaids; Harry Scott and Maurice, groomsmen; and the ceremony was to take place in the house, according to a whim of the bride, who did not choose to exhibit her own and her friends' pretty dresses in the church - "a great ugly barn."

Lucia had also a daily visit to Mr. Leigh to occupy her. He was recovering from his slight attack of illness, and enjoyed her lively talk and affectionate care. One day he even let her persuade him to walk, with her assistance, as far as the Cottage; and when she had established him in the most comfortable chair beside her mother, he was so content with the change that Maurice, coming home from Cacouna, was met by the unheard-of announcement, "Mr. Leigh is out."

He followed the truant, and found him in no hurry to return. The two elder people, indeed, both enjoyed this visit, which seemed to carry them back to a time brighter than the present. They talked of trifles, but of trifles which were in a kind of harmony with the happier days of both. Lucia, sitting at the door, where she could see the sunny landscape and the river, listened idly to their talk, but mixed it with her own girlish fancies; while near to her Maurice sat down, glad of the homelike rest of the moment, glad of the friendly look of welcome with which she met him; knowing distinctly that if at that moment he had asked her for anything more than friendship, she would have been shocked and distressed, but willing to enjoy to the utmost all the happiness her present and grateful regard could give him. Not that he was content; an unspeakable longing to get rid of all this veil of reserve, to make her understand what she was so blind to, to carry her off from all the frivolities which came between them, and make her love him as he thought she might love, lay deep down in his heart and swelled up, at times almost uncontrollably. But she never guessed it, and never should, unless, perhaps, time should bring her a harder discipline than his. Then, if ever she came to want love, to want happiness, it would be his opportunity; at present, he could still wait.

This evening might well be one of enjoyment. It was the last that those four were ever to spend together at the Cottage. Nearly a fortnight had passed since Mr. Bellairs and his cousin had started for Sault Ste. Marie, and they were expected back in a day or two. The preparations for Bella's marriage were almost completed, and Lucia was looking forward with a pleasant flutter of excitement to her own appearance as bridesmaid. Mrs. Costello's letter to Mr. Strafford remained unanswered, but from the circuitous route by which their communication now took place that was not wonderful; rather, indeed, the fact of having heard nothing from him seemed reassuring, and in the interval, no further incident had occurred to disturb her tranquillity. Thus the hours that Maurice and his father spent together at the Cottage were, to the whole party, hours of a certain calm and peace, pleasant to recollect after the calm had been broken.

The next day Lucia spent almost entirely at Mrs. Bellairs'. Bella drove her home in the evening, and when she came in she found Maurice alone on the verandah. It was quite dusk, very nearly dark - a soft, still, dewy evening, and she could but just distinguish his figure as he moved, to meet her.

"Is it you, Maurice?" she said. "Is mamma there?"

"Yes, and no," he answered; "Mrs. Costello is just gone in."

"How is Mr. Leigh? I have not seen him to-day."

"No; I have been at home most of the day."

"Is he worse then?" she said, alarmed.

"He is not quite so well, but nothing serious. Are you tired?"

"No, not at all. Something is the matter, Maurice. I can hear it in your voice."

"Nothing is the matter, I assure you. Something unexpected has happened, but only to my father and me, and I want to talk to you about it. That is all."

"Something unexpected? What?"

"Come down to the river side; it is quiet there and cool."

They went down together; it was growing very dark, and the turf on the bank was soft and uneven. Lucia put her hand through Maurice's arm with her old childlike familiarity, and said,

"Why do you excite my curiosity if you don't mean to satisfy it, you tiresome Maurice?"

"Are you in such a hurry to hear my news, then? I feel in no such haste to tell it. Look, do you see those lights on the river?"

"Yes. How quickly they move! What are they?"

"What we very seldom see here. They are the lights Indians use in spearing fish."

"Indians!"

Lucia's voice was faint, and she clung to Maurice's arm. Surprised to feel her trembling, he said, "I intended a night or two ago to tell you to look out for them. Surely, you are not afraid of an Indian?"

"I am a little," she answered, trying to overcome her terror. "But where do these come from?"

"You know the saw-mill at the other end of the town, beyond Mr. Bayne's? There are three or four Indians at work there, and they go out sometimes at night to fish."

The two lights, which had been but just visible when they first came out, flitting here and there through the darkness, had now approached much nearer, so that the canoes could be plainly distinguished. They were quite small, and each contained two men, one sitting down in the stern, a dark undefined shadow, scarcely seen except for the occasional flash of his paddle in the light; the other standing at the prow in the full glare of the fire which burned there, and lit up his wild half-naked figure and the long fish-spear in his hand. As the canoe moved from place to place, they could see the spear dart swiftly into the water, and the sparkle of wet scales as the fish was brought up and thrown into the boat.

Lucia's terror had at first overpowered her curiosity, and as it subsided, she was, for a minute or two, too much interested in the novel sight to renew her questions. As for Maurice, he was, as he had said, in no haste to speak.

It was pleasant to have her for a little while all to himself, pleasant to feel her hand resting more closely on his arm as if he could protect her, even from her own foolish fear, and all was the sweeter, because it might be for the last time. At last, however, she said again,

"But tell me what you were going to. What has happened?"

"One thing that has happened," he replied, rousing himself, "is that I have heard more family history than I knew before. Do you care to hear that?"

"Yes; I should like to if you don't mind."

"Well, you know that my father and mother came out here from England many years ago, directly after their marriage. This marriage, it appears, was disapproved of by my mother's family - was a runaway match, indeed, and never forgiven even to the time of her death."

"Oh, Maurice! and were her father and mother alive?"

"Her father was, and still is. She was an only daughter, with but one brother; and my grandfather, who is a Norfolk gentleman of large property, expected her, reasonably enough, to marry a man who was her equal in fortune. However, she chose to marry my father, who was then a soldier, a poor lieutenant, with little money, and equally little prospect of rising. I don't know whether women are very wise or very foolish, Lucia, but they seem to see things with different eyes to men. My mother chose to marry, then, though my father was poor, and certain to remain so; though she was a gay spoiled girl of just twenty-one, and he a grave man not much under forty. He sold out, and they came here. I don't believe she ever was unhappy, or repented her marriage, and my father while she lived had all he cared for; since her death, indeed, there has been sorrow after sorrow."

Maurice stopped a moment.

"But you know all that," he said hastily, and went on. "My mother wrote several times to her father and to her brother, first after her arrival in Canada, then after the birth of her eldest child, and last of all just before she died; but no answer ever came. After her death my father, as she wished, wrote again, but until this morning he had heard nothing from my grandfather for all these six-and-twenty years."

"You have heard, then, at last?"

"At last. This morning a letter came. It is a pitiful one to read. My grandfather is, as you may suppose, a very old man; he is ill and alone, and begins to repent, I think, of his harshness to my mother."

"But why is he alone? You said he had a son."

"Yes, but he is dead. He died six months ago, and left but one child, a daughter, who is married and has no children."

"No children? and your grandfather is very rich?"

"I believe so."

"But you are his heir, then? Is that it?"

"He says so, or rather, he says my mother's eldest son is his heir. He knows nothing of me individually."

"And you are the only one left? Ah, Maurice, if Alice even had been alive!"

Maurice sighed.

"If poor Herbert had been alive, how gladly I would have left the heirship to him!"

"But why? I think that is foolish. It is a good thing to be rich. It will be a good thing for you, because you are good."

Maurice laughed.

"Your flattery, Lucia, will not reconcile me to my fate. You have not yet heard all."

"What else? Is Mr. Leigh pleased?"

"Not more than I am. My grandfather wants to see his heir."

"Do you mean that he wants you to go to England?"

"Yes. And my father consents."

"But not yet?"

"At once. To sail from New York on Saturday."

"It is Wednesday now."

"I start to-morrow night."

"When will you come back?"

"When, indeed? Lucia, do not you see that this is a heavy price to pay?"

"Ah! don't go. This grandfather has been cruel all these years; let him wait now. Beside, what will Mr. Leigh do without you?"

"He insists upon my going. He believes it would have been my mother's wish, and therefore he will rather stay here alone than refuse."

"Then you *must* go. But could not you persuade him to come and stay with us? Mamma would like it, I know."

"Impossible, dear child. Who knows how long I may be away, or what changes may take place before I come back."

"Well, we shall see him every day, in any case. But what shall I do without you? and mamma?"

"You remind me of the last thing I have to say. It seems to me, I cannot tell you why, as if this change in my own life was to be followed by other changes. I think Mrs. Costello has something of the same feeling, and I want to say this to you, that if you should find it true, you may remember in any disturbance of this quiet life of yours that I had some vague anticipation of it, and not hesitate to let me be any help, any use, to you that I can be. Do you understand? I shall be away, but I shall not be changed in anything. You told me the other day I always came to your help in your dilemmas. I want you to think of me always so. Can you manage to keep such, a living recollection of the absent?"

Lucia's tears were falling fast by this time in the darkness, yet she thought there was something cold and restrained in Maurice's words and tone, and she could not guess how much the restraint cost him.

"As if I should forget you!" she said rather resentfully. "I could just as soon forget my brother, if I had one."

The word did not suit Maurice. He sighed, with a kind

of impatience.

"Shall we go in?" he said.

They turned towards the house, but when they reached it, instead of following Lucia in, he said "Good-night."

She turned in surprise.

"But you are coming in?"

"Not to-night; my father will be waiting for me."

"Let me call mamma, then."

"I have said good-night to her. You will not forget? I do not mean forget me, but, forget that wherever I am, or wherever you are, you have the right to ask anything of me that a friend can do for you."

"But we shall see you to-morrow?"

"Certainly. Go in; the air is damp and cold."

He went away quickly, but Lucia lingered on the verandah until Mrs. Costello came to look for her. Already she thought the house looked desolate. What should they do without Maurice? Never in her life had she been so sorrowful, yet she had not the slightest idea how far his pain exceeded hers, or how he had longed for a word from her which would have encouraged him, at this last moment, to say all that was in his heart.

CHAPTER VII

When Lucia awoke next morning, her first thought was of Maurice - what should she do without him? She rose and dressed hastily, fancying that at any moment he might come in, and anxious to lengthen, by every means, the time of their nearness to each other.

Maurice, however, though he looked wishfully at the Cottage as he went about his preparations, had too many things to think of and arrange, to steal a moment for the indulgence of his inclinations until afternoon, and she was obliged to wait with such patience as she could for his coming. He had told Mrs. Costello that it would be needful for him to spend two or three hours in Cacouna, and asked her to see his father in the meantime. Thus, in the afternoon, Lucia was for a considerable time quite alone.

Mrs. Costello, meanwhile, with more than friendly sympathy, heard from Mr. Leigh his reasons for urging upon Maurice this hasty departure, and cheered him with anticipations of his speedy return. They consulted over, and completed together, some last preparations for his voyage; and while they felt almost equally the trial of parting with him, the grief of each was a kind of solace to the other. For, in fact, whatever they might say, neither regarded this journey as an ordinary one, or thought that the return they spoke of would be what they tried to imagine it.

Mr. Leigh, believing that his strength was really failing more and more, hastened his son's departure, that the voyage might be made before his increasing weakness should set it aside; his parting from Maurice, therefore, he dreaded as a final one. Mrs. Costello had vaguer, but equally oppressive forebodings. She saw that in all probability a few weeks longer would find her peaceful home deserted, and herself and Lucia fugitives. Even if Maurice, transported into a new world with new interests and incalculably brighter prospects, should still retain his affection for them - and *that* she scarcely doubted - how could he ever again be to them what he had been? far less, what she had hoped he might be?

When Maurice returned, earlier than they expected, from the town, he found them still together. Mrs. Costello soon rose to return home, having seen to the last possible arrangement for the traveller's comfort. He proposed to accompany her, and say good-bye to Lucia, and they left the house together.

"I want to ask you to do me another kindness yet," he said, as soon as they had left the house. "My father, I am sure, will not tell me the truth about himself; he will be terribly lonely, and I am afraid of his health suffering more than it has done. He thinks it a duty to my mother, that I should go to England now; but it will certainly be my duty to him to come back, at all risks, if he feels my being away as much as I fear he will."

"You may at least depend upon one thing," she answered, "we will do all we can to take care of him."

"Thank you, that I know. But, Mrs. Costello, I should be so glad if you would write to me, and so give me the comfort of knowing exactly how he is."

"Certainly I will. You shall have a regular bulletin every mail if you like."

"Indeed, I should like it. And you will send me news also of yourself?"

Mrs. Costello sighed.

"I am forgetting," she said, "and making promises I may not be able to keep. I do not know how long I may be here, or where I may be three months hence."

Maurice looked at her in surprise. That she, who for twelve years had never quitted her home for a single night, should speak thus of leaving it without visible cause or preparation, seemed almost incredible.

She answered his look.

"Yes, I am serious. A dreadful trouble is threatening me, and to save myself and Lucia, I may have to go away. No one knows anything of it. Now that you are leaving us, I dare say so much to you."

"This, then, is why you have changed so, lately? Could not you have trusted me before?"

"It would have been useless; no one can help me."

Her voice seemed changed and broken, and she had grown ashy pale in alluding to the dreadful subject. Maurice could not bear to leave her in this uncertainty.

"Dear Mrs. Costello," he said, "if you had a son you would let him share your anxieties. I have so long been used to think of you almost as a mother, that I feel as if I had a kind of right to your confidence; and I cannot imagine any trouble in which you would be better without friends than with them."

"Sometimes," she answered, "it is part of our penalty to suffer alone. Hitherto I have done so. No, Maurice, though you could scarcely be dearer to me if you were my son, I cannot tell even you, at present, what I fear."

"At present? But you will, later?"

"Later, perhaps. Certainly, if ever we meet again."

"Which we shall do. You do not mean that you would not let me know where you go?"

"Perhaps I ought to mean it."

"It would be useless. Whenever you go I shall find you. You know - I am almost sure you know - that whether right or wrong, it is leaving you that troubles me now, even more than leaving my father."

Mrs. Costello smiled faintly.

"You do me justice," she said, "but I will alter your sentence a little for you, and say that you leave as much of your heart in my house as in your father's. I believe that; I am almost sorry now to believe it."

"Why should you be sorry? Do you think that there is no chance that in time things may be more hopeful for me than they are at present?"

"More hopeful for both our wishes, you might say; but, Maurice, my day-dreams of many years past may have to be given up with my dear little home."

"Do not say so, if, indeed, your wishes are the same as mine. I have faith in time and patience."

"Do not let us say more on the subject - it is too tempting. I, too, must try to have faith in time."

"And you will write to me regularly?"

"As long as I am here."

"And remember that I am not to be shaken off. I belong to you; and you are never to trust anybody else to do a thing for you which I could have done. You will promise me that, won't you?"

"My dear boy, don't make me regret your going more than I should do. In any case, I shall miss you daily."

They had reached the Cottage, and Lucia came out to meet them.

"How slowly you came!" she cried. "I thought you never meant to arrive. Mamma, you look dreadfully tired. What have you been doing to her, Maurice?"

She was talking fast, to keep, if possible, their attention from herself; for, to confess the truth, she had been indulging in a little cry all alone, and did not care that her red eyelids should betray her; but she might have spared the trouble. No word or look of hers was likely to pass unnoticed in that last precious few minutes, though they all sat down together, and tried to talk of indifferent matters as if there had been the least possibility, just then, of any other thought than that of parting.

After a short time, Maurice rose.

"I must give my father the last hour," he said, "and the boat is due at six."

"But it does not ever leave before seven," Lucia answered, "and it is still a quarter to five."

"I have to meet it when it comes in. Mr. Bellairs is coming home by it, and I have various affairs to settle with him."

He looked at her as he said "Mr. Bellairs is coming," but there was no tell-tale change in her face; she had for the moment utterly forgotten Mr. Percy.

"If he had not been coming, you would have had to wait for him, I suppose?" she asked. "I wish he would stay away."

"There are, unfortunately, such things as posts and telegraphs even further west than Cacouna. I sent a telegram to meet him yesterday morning."

"Ah, yes, I suppose where there's a will there's a way."

She spoke pettishly, and he only answered by coming across and holding out his hand to say good-bye. She rose and put out both hers, intending to say, as she often did when she had been cross, "Don't be angry, Maurice, I did not mean it," but the words would not come. Her courage suddenly gave way, and she cried with all her heart.

At that moment Maurice felt that she was really his; he longed unspeakably to claim her once and for ever; but his old generous self-repression was too strong for the temptation, and he shrunk from taking advantage of her grief and her sisterly affection. But a brother has some privileges, and those he had a right to. Her face was hidden, but he bent down, and drawing away her hands for a moment, kissed her with something more than a brother's warmth, pressed Mrs. Costello's hand, and hurried away.

Lucia listened intently as the sound of his footsteps, and of the gate as he passed through it, died away. Then she raised her head, and pushing back her hair, came and sat down at her mother's feet, hiding her flushed face and laughing a little half hysterical laugh.

But the laugh was a complete failure, and broke down into a sob, which was followed by a great many others, enough to have satisfied Maurice himself. At last she checked herself. "What a baby I am!" she said.

Mrs. Costello stroked back gently the soft black locks which were falling loose over her lap.

"You are a child, Lucia. I have never been in any haste for you to be otherwise."

Mrs. Harry Coghill

"But I am not such a child, really, mamma. Sixteen and a half! I ought to be very nearly a woman."

Mrs. Costello sighed.

"You will be a woman soon enough, my darling, be content as to that."

"All the sooner now I have nobody but you to keep me in order. Mamma, how *shall* we do without Maurice at Bella's wedding?"

When the 'Queen of the West' passed down the river that evening with Maurice on board, he could plainly distinguish two figures standing on the verandah of the Cottage, and recognize Mrs. Costello's black dress, and Lucia's softly flowing muslin, framed in the green branches of the vine and climbing roses. One of those roses went with him on his journey to remind him, if anything were needed to remind him, of the place to which, even more than to his father's house, his heart turned as home.

For a whole day Lucia had scarcely once remembered Mr. Percy; and that same day she had scarcely been a moment absent from his thoughts. Not that this had been at all the case during the whole of his absence from Cacouna. On the contrary, he had, in spite of his ill-humour at starting, found so many agreeable distractions in the course of his journey that, at the end of a week, he congratulated himself on being entirely cured of a very foolish and troublesome fancy. No sooner, however, had they begun their return - taking, it is true; a different route, and continuing to visit new places - than it appeared that the cure was not yet entirely complete; still he paid little attention to the returning symptoms, and suffered them to increase unchecked till, at the commencement of their last day's journey, the magnet had resumed all its former power, and he became positively impatient to find himself again at the Cottage.

Mr. Percy was not by any means so much in love as to be blind to the extreme inconvenience and impolicy of anything like a serious love affair with a little Canadian girl such as Lucia Costello; but in the meantime she attracted him delightfully, and he always trusted to good luck for some means of extrication, if matters should go a step further than he intended. As for the possibility of her suffering, that did not enter into his calculations; there would, of course, be some tears, and she would look prettier than ever through them; but women always shed tears and always wipe them away again, and forget them. So he came back quite prepared to enjoy the two or three weeks which still remained to him, by spending as many hours daily, as possible, in pursuit of what he knew at the bottom of his heart he neither expected nor wished to retain, when it was once gained.

The pleasure of rivalling and mortifying Maurice had been, at first, one of Percy's strongest incentives in his attentions to Lucia; and as he found that, do what he could, it was impossible to force "that young Leigh" to *show* either jealousy or mortification, he began to hate him. He had enough sense and tact not to betray this feeling either to Mrs. Costello or Lucia, but it only grew stronger for being repressed. Mr. Bellairs, for some reason, said nothing to his cousin of the telegram he received from Maurice at the town where they spent the last night of their tour; it was, therefore, without any idea of what had really happened that he perceived the father and son standing together on the wharf as the boat drew towards it. But as soon as he understood the cause of their being there, it occurred to him that this chance interview would be useful to him at the Cottage; he knew enough of women to guess that the smallest scrap of information about the traveller, even to be able to say, "I saw him on board the boat," would make him additionally welcome to them. Accordingly, he spoke to Maurice with more civility than usual, inquired to what part of England he was going, and gave him, in his usual lazy fashion, some information about railways and hotels which was likely to be useful to a stranger in the country. Having thus not only done himself good, but as he felt, displayed a most courteous and charitable spirit, he left Mr. Bellairs with the Leighs and walked up to the house, where Bella's bridal preparations had been going on vigorously during his absence.

These preparations were nearly finished, for only three days remained before that fixed for the wedding; and all had gone on smoothly, until the sudden news of Maurice's summons to England deranged the bridal party, and threw the bride into a fit of ill-humour from which Doctor Morton was the greatest sufferer. She would not be satisfied with any substitute either he or her sister could propose, and was the more unreasonable because she knew that when her brother-in-law (of whom she had really some little awe) should arrive, she would have to lay aside her whims, and consent to accept whoever could be found to take the office of groomsman at so short a notice. When he came, accordingly, she was quite silent and submissive - a short consultation ended in what she had expected; and Mr. Percy took Maurice's place in the programme. Neither Mr. nor Mrs. Bellairs were altogether pleased that it should be so, but they comforted themselves with the idea that he would very shortly be leaving Canada, and that as he and Lucia would necessarily see much of each other while he did remain at Cacouna, their being associated together on that one day could not be of any great consequence.

The next morning, therefore, when Mr. Percy made his appearance at the Cottage, he had much to tell. But Lucia was still thinking more of Maurice than of him; she was unusually quiet, and more inclined to talk of England and to learn all she could of the voyage thither and of the journey from Liverpool to Norfolk, than to occupy herself either with the wedding or with the incidents of his tour on the Lakes. For the first time Mr. Percy was alarmed; he began to think it possible that during his absence, Maurice had so well used his time as to deprive him of the influence which he had before acquired over Lucia's mind; and this idea caused him suddenly to fancy that it was absolutely necessary to his happiness that he should displace Maurice altogether from her thoughts, even if, to do so, he should have to devote himself to her in the most serious earnest.

So Mr. Bellairs' stratagem failed. Before the two days, with their constant comings and goings, were over, Mrs. Costello saw, with dismay, that not only was Mr. Percy so far awakened from his usual state of boredom as to be one of the most dangerous flatterers imaginable to a girl of sixteen, but that Lucia appeared to have yielded completely to an attraction which had now no counterpoise, since Maurice had left them.

Each day Lucia spent as long a time as she could with Mr. Leigh, and strangely enough, the old man seemed to feel less depression after Maurice was actually gone, than he had done in anticipating the separation. In the hours which Lucia passed with him, he took delight in talking to her of his wife, and her early home, describing it with that wonderful recollection of trifles which seems to return to old people when they speak of the incidents and scenes of their youth. And Lucia loved to listen, and to picture to herself Maurice making acquaintance with all these things which his father spoke of; and becoming necessary to the proud, childless possessor of such wealth and so fair a home, just as he had been necessary to them all, far away in the west. After all, these hours were the happiest of Lucia's life at that time. They brought her the consciousness of doing right - of doing what would please Maurice, whose approbation had, all her life, been one of her dearest rewards for "being good;" and she had also the actual enjoyment of these quiet conversations, coming in, as they did, between the more vivid and more troubled delights of feeling herself engrossed by a spell, to whose power she submitted with joy indeed, but also with trembling. Every time she now saw Bella, it appeared to her more entirely incomprehensible that any one could act as she was doing; the mere idea of a marriage where convenience, suitableness, common sense were the best words that could be used to account for it, began to seem revolting. She could not have explained why, yet she felt, at times, a positive repugnance to take any part in the celebration of so worldly, so loveless a contract.

It was in this humour that she came back from Cacouna the evening before the wedding. Bella had been more flippant than usual, until even Mrs. Bellairs had completely lost patience with her, and the incorrigible girl had only been stopped by the fear of her guardian's displeasure from insisting on driving Lucia home, while Doctor Morton, who had been all day absorbed by his patients, waited for her decision about some arrangements for their journey. Lucia could not help giving her what Bella called a lecture, but when she reached home and was seated in her usual place at her mother's feet, she was still puzzling over the subject, and over what Mrs. Costello had said when she first heard of the engagement.

"Mamma," she said, at last, "do you remember saying you thought Bella's might be a very happy marriage? I wonder if you think so still?"

"Why should not I? What is changed?"

"I don't know that anything is; but you know how tiresome she is. I cannot imagine how Doctor Morton bears it."

"Probably, he bears it because he thinks her tiresomeness will soon be over. When she is married and in her own house, she will have other things to think of besides teasing him."

"But, mamma, do you think she *loves* him?"

Mrs. Costello laughed. "Indeed, my dear, I can't tell. If she does not now, I suppose she intends to."

"But that can't be right. Mamma, I am certain you do not think that kind of marriage right."

"Not for all people, certainly. But for any one who is dear to me I would far rather have a marriage of 'that kind' than one founded on the hasty, utterly unreasonable fancy which girls often call love."

Lucia blushed crimson, but would not give up her point. "I am sure if I married a man I did not love, I should hate him in three months," she said.

"I do not think you and Bella are much alike," Mrs. Costello answered; "and as for her, perhaps it may comfort you to know that I have speculated a little on this subject, and I have some suspicion that there may be more sentiment in the affair then she allows."

Lucia started up. "Really, mamma, I am so glad," she cried. "Only, why should she be so stupid?"

"I don't think even you, Lucia, would be pleased to see Bella and Doctor Morton enacting the same *role* as Magdalen and Harry Scott."

"I am sure I should not. It would be too ridiculous. But just look at Mr. and Mrs. Bellairs, *they* seem perfectly happy; and Mr. and Mrs. Leigh must have been so, in spite of everything. Maurice told me he believed his mother had never regretted her marriage; and that was certainly a love match."

"Mine was a 'love match,' Lucia, and brought me misery unimaginable. Hush, say no more at present."

CHAPTER VIII

Bella's wedding-day rose as fair and bright as a day could be. The waning summer seemed to have returned to the freshness of early June, and to have determined that the bride, whatever else might be wanting, should have all the blessing sunshine could give her. Lucia, however, after that first eager look out at the weather which we naturally give on the morning of a fete-day, began to be conscious of a mood far too depressed and uneasy to be in harmony with either the weather or the occasion. Partly perhaps it was that her eyes had turned from habit to Maurice's window, which when he was at home was always open early, but whose closed up, solitary look now, reminded her of his absence; partly that the words her mother had spoken the previous evening lingered in her mind, and not only brought back more forcibly than ever all her puzzled and anxious thought about the past and future, but seemed to throw a dark but impalpable cloud over the happiness of the present.

But there was too much business to be done for her to spend time in dreaming, and by the time she was ready for breakfast, the inclination to dream had almost past away. After breakfast, and after the various daily affairs which in the small household fell to her share to attend to, there were flowers to be gathered, and a short visit to Mr. Leigh to be paid; and by the time all this was done, it was time to dress.

If this dressing was a longer process than usual, and if Lucia was a little fanciful and hard to please over it, no one need be surprised. Everybody knows that at a wedding, the bridesmaids rank next in importance to the bride, and far before the bridegroom, who, for that day at least, sinks into the most miserable insignificance. But it was not only a perfect consciousness of the place in the eyes of the multitude which she was expected to fill that made Lucia whimsical; much stronger than even that, was the desire to please one, - the shy wish to be admired, to see that she was so, possibly to hear it. She wondered to herself whether she would look very awkward and rustic beside Lord Lastingham's handsome daughters, and whether a certain Lady Adeliza, whose name had somehow reached her ears, was much more beautiful than she could ever hope to be. Poor child! her uneasiness on that point would certainly have ceased if she could have peeped into Mr. Percy's brain and seen the two portraits he carried about with him there, - herself fresh and lovely as Psyche when she captivated Love himself, and Lady Adeliza, highly distinguished and a little faded, but, for a poor man, a very desirable match. She would have failed, probably, to understand that last qualification, or to guess how it could completely outweigh youth, beauty, and love, together; and so would have felt even more joyous and less diffident than she did, when at last the important business was finished, and she stepped into the carriage which was to take her to Mrs. Bellairs'.

There she found Bella, for once tolerably subdued, and submitting with more patience than anybody expected of her, to be dressed by her sister and Magdalen Scott. The moment she saw Lucia, however, she whirled herself round out of their hands, and vowed she would not do another thing until she had had time to look at her bridesmaids both together.

"You are perfectly charming!" she exclaimed, holding up her hands in mock ecstasy. "It's quite useless for me to dress, Elise. Who will look at me when they are to be seen?"

"Don't be absurd, Bella. It is time you were ready now."

"I'm in despair, my dear. Give me any shabby old dress, and

here, Lucia, put this thing on, and be the bride instead of me."

She caught up her veil and threw it over Lucia's head before any one could stop her.

"You must change the bridegroom as well then," said Magdalen, rather maliciously, "and perhaps she might not object."

"What a pity Maurice is gone! It will have to be Mr. Percy, Lucia," cried Bella, loosing the veil to clap her hands.

"Be silent, Bella," said Mrs. Bellairs, "and finish dressing at once, unless you intend me to leave you."

Lucia, flushed and half angry, had by this time freed herself from the veil and smoothed her hair. Bella, a little sobered by her sister's annoyance, returned to her toilette and was soon ready to go downstairs.

In the drawing-room the guests were rapidly assembling. A space near one end had been kept clear, but every other corner soon filled; and the party overflowed into Mrs. Bellairs' own little room adjoining. Mr. And Mrs. Bayne were among the last arrivals, and punctual to the appointed time came the bridegroom and Harry Scott.

A little change and flutter of the colour on Bella's cheek, when the well-known knock was heard, showed that she was not entirely without trepidation, but she rose quietly, took a last look at herself in the glass, and was standing ready when her brother-in law came to fetch her. In the hall, the bridegroom and his two friends met them - the drawing-room door opened, and, with a soft rustle and gleam of white dresses, the little party passed up through the crowd, and took their places before the clergyman.

There was no want of seriousness in Bella now. She had become so extremely pale that Mrs. Bellairs watched her anxiously; but except that her responses were made in a perfectly clear and audible tone, without the smallest tremulousness, or appearance of what one of her neighbours called "proper feeling," she was a most exemplary bride - even to the point of looking prettier than she had ever been known to do before, and almost eclipsing her bridesmaids. But, the ceremony over, she did not remain long so unlike herself. She was quiet, certainly, but as gay, mischievous, and childish as ever.

Breakfast followed the marriage almost immediately. It was, of course, as brilliant an affair as the resources of Cacouna could produce, and everybody really seemed to enjoy themselves. The newly-married pair were in all eyes but Lucia's so well and happily matched, and had so reasonable a prospect of being content with each other and their fortunes, that there did not seem to be a single cloud on the day. The same boat which had carried Maurice away three days before, took the bride and bridegroom on their tour, and not long after, the guests who had dispersed after breakfast began to reassemble for the evening dance. Lucia and Magdalen, at the window of what had been Bella's room, amused themselves by watching the arrivals and talking over the event of the morning.

"Did you ever see such a girl as Bella?" said Magdalen. "It seems as if she could never be serious for a moment. She went off laughing as if she were just coming back in half an hour."

"Why should not she? She is not going away as some people do, hundreds of miles from all her old friends."

"No, but then it must be a kind of parting; she will never be with her sister again as she used to be. I am sure I should have cried. There is something dreadful in it, I think. It seems like leaving all one's youth behind."

Magdalen sighed rather affectedly. Lucia laughed.

"People should not marry till they are old, according to that. I don't quite believe you think so, however. But, you know,

Bella always declared a bride ought not to cry. I wonder if she will be any graver now she is Mrs. Morton?"

"What do you think Harry says about the doctor?"

"What?"

"He says Bella will find a difference between him and her guardian. Mr. Bellairs used to let her spend her money just as she liked, and give away a great deal, but Doctor Morton looks too sharply after the dollars and cents for that. He never lets himself be cheated out of a farthing, and never gives anything away."

"I don't like people who are quite so careful, to be sure; but Bella used to be rather extravagant sometimes."

"Indeed she was. I can't think how she will do, so good-natured as she is, if her husband is so dreadfully hard."

"Perhaps Harry is mistaken, though. Come, we must go down."

"You will have to dance Maurice's quadrille with Mr. Percy to-night, Lucia; are not you sorry?"

Lucia blushed. "Poor Maurice!" she said, and they went downstairs. Magdalen was right. Lucia danced with Percy, and thought no more of Maurice. The evening passed too quickly; it seemed as if so much happiness ought to last, but twelve o'clock came, and the elder people began to disappear. Mrs. Bellairs had left the room where the dancers were for a few minutes, and Lucia found her, looking tired and worried, in a small one which was quite deserted.

"I think I ought to go home," she said. "It is getting late. But, dear Mrs. Bellairs, how dreadfully tired you look!"

"I am tired; but weddings don't happen very often. Have you

been enjoying yourself?"

"Oh! yes, so much. I don't think there ever was such a delightful party. It is only a pity Bella could not be here, and Maurice."

"I am afraid Maurice would not have enjoyed himself so much as you have done. Lucia, I am a little vexed with you, though I do not know whether I ought to say so."

Lucia hung her head for a moment, and then raised it saucily, confident that, as she stood half in shadow, her glowing cheeks could not be seen.

"Why are you vexed with me?" she asked.

But it was not so easy to answer the question straightforwardly, andMrs. Bellairs paused, half repenting that she had spoken.

"Do you know," she said, "what people are beginning to call you? They say that you are a flirt; and that is not a desirable character for a girl to acquire."

Lucia's cheeks burned in good earnest now, but it was with anger, not shame.

"But it is not true. I am not a flirt. It is quite absurd to say so. You know I am not, Mrs. Bellairs."

She was right. This was not at all the accusation which her friend had in her heart to make, though people *did* say it, and Mrs. Bellairs had heard them.

Lucia turned around. "I will get ready to go," she said. But some one was standing close beside her.

"Mr. Percy!" she exclaimed angry and annoyed, while Mrs. Bellairs hastily congratulated herself that he had neither been mentioned nor alluded to.

"I beg your pardon," he said. "I came in this instant to look for you for our waltz. Some one told me you were here."

But Lucia could not recover her temper in a moment.

"It is very late," she said, "and I am too tired to dance any more - pray excuse me;" and she walked out of the room with the most dignified air in the world, leaving Mr. Percy in considerable surprise and some offence. There was something so charming, however, in her little air of pride and displeasure, that he admired her more then ever; while she, quite unconscious of the effect her ill-humour had produced, made haste to prepare for her drive home, but found an opportunity at the last moment to throw her arms round Mrs. Bellairs' neck and whisper, as she said good-night,

"Don't be vexed with me. Indeed I shall never be a flirt."

As usual, on Lucia's return from any evening amusement, Mrs. Costello herself opened the door of the Cottage on her arrival. They went together to the parlour for a few minutes, and afterwards to Lucia's room, but it was not until her mother left her that it struck the poor child that some new alarm or distress had happened.

"I shall not go to sleep," she said to herself, "but wait and ask mamma when she comes in;" but youth and fatigue were too strong for her resolution, and she was soon fast asleep. It was not, indeed, till dawn that Mrs. Costello came; her night had been spent like so many before it, in painful thought and vigil; but before she slept, she had, as she hoped, fixed clearly and definitely her plans for the future. To have done this, was in itself a kind of relief. She slept at last calmly, and woke in the morning with a sensation of certainty and renewed courage, which she had long been without.

At breakfast she was so cheerful and had so many questions to ask about the previous day, that Lucia readily persuaded herself that she had no need to be uneasy.

She did indeed say, "Have you heard from Mr. Strafford?" but Mrs. Costello's answer satisfied her: "I had a note yesterday evening. He is coming up, and may be here to-morrow," and no more was said.

She found when she went over, soon after breakfast, to Mr. Leigh's, that the post of the evening before had brought him also a letter, full of interest to them all. It was from Maurice; and though it only described his journey to New York, his stay there, and the steamer in which he had taken his passage for England, it seemed for the moment almost to bring him back home. They lingered over it, as people do over the first letter, and amused themselves by guessing how far he could yet be on his voyage; whether the weather, which at Cacouna had been fair and calm, would have been good or bad for those far out on the Atlantic. That day neither Lucia nor Mr. Leigh cared for newspaper or book. They had plenty to talk about, for when the subject of the letter was completely finished, there still remained the wedding, of which Mr. Leigh said Maurice would be sure to demand a full account. So they talked hour after hour, and forgot how time was going, until Mrs. Costello, growing uneasy, came to look for her daughter, and found them still absorbed in their gossip.

But when the afternoon began to be almost over, and there had been no other interruptions to their quiet, Lucia found the interest of yesterday worn out, and felt a vague want of something beyond her mother's or Mr. Leigh's companionship. Mr. Percy's usual visit had not been paid, and she could not help wondering whether he stayed away because he was offended with her last night; whether he would come yet, whether he had heard what Mrs. Bellairs had said, or what she answered; and while she wondered, her attention grew so engrossed that she did not hear when her mother spoke to her, until the words had been twice repeated.

Mrs. Costello, at last, touched her arm.

"Are you asleep, Lucia?" she said. "I have spoken to you two or three times already."

"Have you, mamma? I am very sorry. I believe I was half asleep."

"You should have a walk. You have not been further than Mr. Leigh's all day."

"I do not wish to go. I am quite content here, and I will not go to sleep again. Tell me what you were going to say?"

"Something of so little consequence that I have forgotten it. But do go, like a good child, and have a little walk. You must go to-morrow to see Mrs. Bellairs, but to-day I dare say she is glad to be quiet."

Lucia went reluctantly, put on her hat, and started. She was so accustomed to walking alone that she never thought of objecting on that score, and turned, without deliberation, along the road that led to Cacouna. It was a very quiet country road, running along the course of the river; sometimes quite close to the bank, sometimes, as at the Cottage, leaving room for a house and garden. The bank itself was high and generally precipitous, but in some places it sloped more gradually and was covered with soft turf. On the opposite, or American side, the land was lower, and a little of town which lay almost opposite to Cacouna was girdled in on all sides by pine-woods, the tops of which showed like a black fringe against the brilliant light and colour of the sunset sky. This contrast of brightness and darkness in the distance, was heightened by the fainter, but still vivid gleam of the water, as the river, stretching away in an unbroken sheet more than half a mile in width, caught and reflected the changing colours of the clouds. This view, which she had seen daily ever since she could remember, seemed always to possess a new charm for Lucia; whatever might be her humour, it was certain to subside into the same calm and almost reverent attention while she watched the scene reach its most perfect splendour, and then fade softly and gradually into night.

But; at present, it wanted at least half an hour of sunset. There was plenty of time for her walk before the short twilight would begin. She strolled on, rather pleased to be alone, and in no hurry to traverse the space of lonely road which intervened between Mr. Leigh's and the first houses of the town. As she had expected, there was not a single passenger on the way, nor did she see any one until, just as the first roof began to be visible in front of her, she perceived lying by the roadside what looked like a large bundle of old clothes. Coming nearer, she found that it was a man apparently fast asleep, his head hidden by his arms. Suspecting him, from his attitude, to be tipsy, she felt for a moment inclined to turn back, but her hesitation seemed so foolish that it was immediately conquered, and, keeping on the opposite side, she walked quietly past. She had scarcely done so, however, when a loud discordant shout was heard from the river, and the sleeper, awakened by it, suddenly raised his head, and began to scramble as quickly as he could to his feet. Lucia hurried on, but in a moment, hearing unsteady footsteps coming fast behind her, and a thick inarticulate voice calling, she turned to look. Scarcely three yards from her, staggering along, and muttering, as if he thought the call which had awakened him was hers, was an Indian, his dark face bloated and brutalized by drink. As she turned, he came nearer and tried to catch her dress. Happily, he was so much intoxicated that she easily evaded his hand, and with a cry of terror fled along the road. But the Indian still pursued, and she was hurrying blindly on, only conscious of that horrible face behind her, and of the failing of her strength from excess of terror, when a voice she knew cried "Lucia!" and she found Mr. Percy by her side.

In another moment her agony of alarm was over; she was standing, still trembling violently, but feeling safe and supported, with her hand drawn firmly through his arm, while her pursuer seemed to have slunk away at the sight of a third person, and was now reeling towards the river bank, whence the same voice as before could be heard calling.

Mr. Percy did not attempt to question or comment. He waited

Mrs. Harry Coghill

patiently till Lucia's panic had subsided and she found voice to say, "Oh! I am so glad you came."

"So am I. What a brute! Yes, I am glad I came just then."

He was so earnest, so shaken out of his usual listless manner, that she was almost startled. It flashed into her mind too how he had cried "Lucia" in a tone which she had heard in her terror without remarking.

"Are you able to walk on now?" he asked, looking at her with real solicitude and anxiety.

"Oh! yes," she answered, and they went on slowly.

"But how did you come?" she inquired after a minute's silence. "The road seemed quite deserted just before."

"I came up from the landing below there. Bellairs persuaded me to go out fishing with him this evening, and as we came back I caught sight of a figure I thought was yours, and made him land me - happily just in time."

"Happily indeed. I did not even see your boat."

"We were too close under the bank most of the time. At the landing, there was a canoe lying, with a man in it, most likely waiting for that brute. You see he is gone down towards it."

Lucia shuddered. "I think I should have fallen down in another minute. I looked round once, and saw such a horrible face, red and swollen and frightful, with the hair all hanging about it. I shall never forget it."

"Don't speak of it at present. You see it is not safe for you to go about alone."

"But I never was frightened before. Now, I believe I shall be, always."

"And I shall not be here again. I was coming to-night to tell you that I am summoned home."

They stopped involuntarily, and their eyes met. There was an equal trouble in both faces. Lucia was the first to recover herself; she made a movement to go on, and tried to speak, but felt instantly that her voice could not be trusted.

Mr. Percy's prudence failed utterly. "I meant to say good-bye" he said, "but it is harder than I thought. I can't leave you here, after all. Lucia, you must come with me."

He was holding her hand, forcing her to stop and to look at him, and finding in her beautiful, innocent face the sweetest excuse a man could have for such madness. Madness it must have been, for he had wholly forgotten himself, and all his life had taught him; and for the moment felt that this girl, who loved him, was worth more than everything else in the world would be without her.

That night Lucia saw nothing of the sunset. Dusk came on, and the fireflies began to flit round them, before the two, who were so occupied with each other, came to the Cottage gate. When they did so, they had yet a few last words to say.

"What will mamma say?" Lucia half whispered. "I am almost afraid to see her."

"Will you tell her or shall I? Which shall you like best? I will come in the morning."

"I shall not sleep to-night if she does not know. I suppose I must tell her, if you will not come in now."

"Not now. I must arrange my thoughts a little first. After all, Lucia, you don't know how little I have to offer you."

"What does that matter?" she asked simply. "Mamma will not care - nor I."

"You will not, of course. You would be content to live like a bird, on next to nothing; but then you know nothing of the world."

"No, indeed. I am nothing better than a baby."

"You are a million times better than any other woman, and will make the best and dearest of wives - if you had only a luckier fellow for a husband."

"Are you unlucky, really? Are you very poor?"

"Poor enough for a hermit. My father is not much richer; and as I have the good fortune to be a younger son, the little he has will go to George, my elder brother, not to me."

Lucia was silent a moment, thinking.

"Are you frightened?" he asked her. "You did not know things were quite so bad?"

"I am not frightened," she answered. "But I was considering. Mamma has some money; she would give me what she could, but I am not like Bella, you know. I have not any fortune at all."

Mr. Percy laughed, "Do not puzzle yourself over such difficulties to-night, at any rate. Leave me to think of those. I will tell you what you must do. Make up your mind to be as charming as possible when you see my father, and fascinate him in spite of himself; for, I assure you he will not very readily forgive us for deranging his plans. Good-night now, I shall be here early to-morrow."

He went away up the lane, while she lingered yet for a moment, looking after him, trying to understand clearly what had happened - to realize this wonderful happiness which was yet only like a dream. How could she go out of the soft summer darkness into the bright light of the parlour and its every day associations? But as she retraced every word and look of the past hour, she came back at last to the horrible recollection of the Indian who had alarmed her. That hideous besotted face seemed to stare at her again through the obscurity, and, trembling with fright, she hurried through the garden and up the verandah steps.

Mrs. Costello was sitting at work by the table where the light fell brightly, but Lucia was glad that the lamp-shade threw most of the room into comparative darkness. Even as it was, she came with shy lingering steps to her mother's side, and was in no hurry to answer her question, "Where have you been loitering so long?"

"I have been at the gate some time," she said. "It is so pleasant out of doors."

"I went to the top of the lane to look for you a long time ago, and saw you coming with, I thought, Mr. Percy."

"Yes. He met me. Mamma, I want to tell you something about - "

Mrs. Costello laid down her work.

"What?" she said almost sharply, as something in her child's soft caressing attitude, and broken words struck her with a new terror.

Lucia slid down to the floor, half kneeling at her mother's feet. "About myself - and him," she murmured.

Mrs. Costello raised her daughter's face to the light, and looked at it closely with an almost bitter scrutiny.

"Child," she said, "I thought you would have been safe from this. I did him injustice, it seems."

A new instinct in Lucia's mind roused her against her mother.

She let her clinging arms fall, and raised her head.

"I do not understand you, mother," she answered, and half rose from where she had been kneeling.

"Stay, Lucia," and her mother's hand detained her. "I have tried to save you from suffering. I see now that I have been wrong. But tell me all."

Awed and startled out of the sweet dreams of a few minutes ago, Lucia tried to obey. She said a few almost unintelligible words, then came to a sudden pause. She had slipped back again to her old place after her little burst of anger, and now looked up pleadingly to her mother.

"But, indeed, I don't know how it was," she said; "only it was after the Indian went away."

Mrs. Costello started. "What Indian?" she asked.

And then the story came out, vivid enough, but broken up as it were by the newer, sweeter excitement of that other story which she could only tell in broken words and blushes. As she spoke her eyes were still raised to her mother's face, looking only for the reflection of her own terror and thankfulness; but she saw such deadly paleness and rigidity steal over it, that she started up in dismay.

Mrs. Costello signed to her to wait, and in a moment was again so far mistress of herself as to be able to say,

"Sit down again. Finish your story, and then describe this man if you can."

Her voice was forced and husky, but Lucia dared not disobey. She had only a few words to add, but her description had nothing characteristic in it, except the utterly degraded and brutal expression of the countenance, which had so vividly impressed her.

When she ceased speaking, both remained for some minutes silent and without moving. Then Mrs. Costello rose, and began to walk slowly up and down the room. She felt that she had made a mistake in the affair nearest to her heart. She knew that Lucia had a girl's fancy for Mr. Percy; he had done all he could to awaken it, and it was not likely that the poor child would have been entirely untouched by his efforts; but she had believed that it was only for the amusement of his leisure that he had been so perseveringly blind to her own coldness, and that he was too thoroughly selfish to be guilty of such an imprudence as she now saw had been committed. That Lucia could ever be his wife, she knew was utterly impossible. She had thought that the worst which could happen, was that when he had left Cacouna his memory would have to be slowly and painfully eradicated from her heart, but now it had become needful to cause this beloved child a double share of the trouble, which she had so dreaded for her. All these thoughts, and with them the idea of an added horror overhanging herself, seemed to press upon her brain with unendurable weight. Yet, suffer as she might, time must not be suffered to pass. Night was advancing, and before morning Lucia must know all the story, which once told, would shadow her life, and throw her new-born happiness out of her very recollection.

She stopped at last in her restless walk. She went up to the chair where Lucia sat, and putting her arms round her, kissed her forehead.

"You are very happy, my child?" she said tenderly.

"Mamma, I don't know. I *was* happy."

"You will be again - not yet, but later. Try to believe that, for it is time you should share my secret and my burden, and they are terrible for you now."

CHAPTER IX

"You will be happy again!" Did any one of us in the first dull pain of a new, inexplicable suffering, ever believe such words as those? Lucia read her mother's face, tone, gestures too well to doubt that she regarded this long-kept secret as something which must separate her from Percy - must separate her, she therefore fancied, from all that was best and sweetest in life. It was hard that she should have been suffered to taste happiness, if it was instantly to be snatched from her. She felt this half resentfully, shrinking into herself, and cowering before the unknown trial, which, when fully understood, her natural courage would enable to meet with energy. She sat with her head resting on her hands, while Mrs. Costello left the room, and came back carrying a small, old-fashioned desk, which she placed upon the table. This desk, which she knew had been her mother's when a girl, and which contained many little treasures, attracted Lucia's attention. Obeying a sign from Mrs. Costello, she came forward, and watched while it was opened, and the many familiar objects taken out. Underneath all, where she had always thought the desk remained empty, the pressure of a spring opened another compartment, in which lay a few papers and a likeness.

"You have often asked me to show you your father's likeness, Lucia," Mrs. Costello said with slow painful utterance. "There it is. Take it, and you will know my secret."

Lucia put out her hand, but as it touched the portrait lying there face downwards, she involuntarily drew it back, and glanced at her mother.

"Must I see it? Must I know?" she whispered tremblingly.

"You must."

She lifted the picture and looked, but the lines swam before her eyes. As they steadied and came out clearly she saw a tall figure with black hair, dressed in a gaily striped shirt and blanket, and leaning on a spear - an Indian. She threw the likeness from her with a cry, "Impossible! It is *not* true," and with clasped hands tried to shut out the hateful sight.

Shudder after shudder swept over her, and still she cried in her heart, "I will not believe it," but she said no more aloud. Her father! All her lifelong terror of his race, all that she had known of them up to the encounter of that very evening, which now seemed years ago, surged through her mind; and, as if mocking her, came above all, her own face with the dark traits which she had believed to be Spanish, but which she could now trace to such a different origin. In a moment, and for ever, her girlish vanity fell from her. She felt as if her beauty were but the badge of degradation and misery. And then there came the keen instinct of resentment - it was to her mother, whom she loved, that she owed this intolerable suffering. Crouching down and shivering, as if with cold, she yielded to the storm of thought which swept over her, yielded to it in a kind of blind despair, from which she had neither wish nor power to rouse herself.

But this mood, which seemed to paralyse her, lasted in reality but a few minutes; she was roused by her mother's voice and touch. She looked up for a moment, but with hard tearless eyes and set lips, and only to put away from her the hand that had been softly laid on her shoulder. Mrs. Costello drew back; she returned to her chair, and sat down to wait, but the long deep sigh which unconsciously escaped her, as she did so, reached Lucia's heart. A strong impulse of love and pity seemed to break through all her misery; she felt that, at least, she did not suffer alone, and with a quick self-reproach she threw herself at her mother's feet, and encircled her waist with her arms. For a moment neither spoke. They held each other fast, and one, at least, thanked God silently that the most bitter pang was averted, since they could still so cling to each other.

But after a while, Mrs. Costello said, "I have much to tell you, my child. Can you bear to hear it now?"

"Yes, mother. I must know all now."

Lucia rose, and bringing a footstool, sat down in her old childish attitude at her mother's feet; only that her face, which was worn and pale, was quite hidden.

"I am ready," she said. "Explain all I cannot understand."

No human being, perhaps, could tell his or her own story with perfect truth; still less could tell it so to the hearer the most passionately loved, and whose love seems to hang in the balance. It would be apt to be a piece of special pleading, for or against, as egotism or conscience happened to be strongest. Best, then, not to try to reproduce the words spoken that night - spoken in the tuneless, level voice, which, in its dull monotony, is a truer indication of pain than any other; but to repeat only the substance of all that Lucia then heard for the first time.

To her, the old house by the Dee was already familiar ground; she knew, dimly, the figure of a lady who died there in her youth, and left a desolate child, well cared for, but little loved, to grow up alone; and she knew, more familiarly, but with a sense of awe which was almost dislike, the child's father, her own grandfather, a man saddened, silent, unsympathetic. These, and various relations and servants who had surrounded her mother in her childhood, she had already heard of a thousand times. The story, new to her, began in Mary Wynter's fifteenth year.

At that time Mr. Wynter's family consisted of four persons - himself, his daughter, her governess, and a nephew, George Wynter, who was, in fact, an adopted son. The governess had been lately and hastily added to the household, on the discovery of Mary's amazing ignorance; and her selection had been a mistake. She and her pupil were at open warfare, she endeavouring to teach, Mary determined not to learn. The poor lady was very conscientious, and very well instructed, but she was not judicious. She never found out that her pupil would have been an absolute slave to affection, but was altogether hardened to severity, and when she failed in herself enforcing her authority, she made the great and most unlucky mistake of appealing to George Wynter. Mary, up to that time, had had no dislike to her cousin. He was nearly twenty years older than herself, an excellent man, who took everything *au pied de la lettre*, and who, perceiving that what Miss Smith said was reasonable, thought duty and common sense required him to "speak to" her *un*reasonable pupil. He never discovered his mistake - nor Miss Smith hers; but things grew more and more uncomfortable. Miss Smith tired of her struggles, and sought more manageable pupils; and Mary, immediately after her fifteenth birthday, was sent to school.

Removed to a new atmosphere, no longer chilled by loneliness or embittered by the consciousness of perpetual disapproval, the girl began to bloom sweetly and naturally. For the first time she was fortunate in her surroundings. Companionship made her gay, and emulation woke keen and successful ambition. Nearly three years passed, and, in place of ignorance and insubordination, she had gained a bright intelligence and a becoming submission. At seventeen she returned home, a girl who would have brought to a mother both pride and anxiety.

But there was no mother to receive her. At the sight of her, her father was a little shaken out of his accustomed thoughts and habits. He tried to imagine what his wife would have done or counselled for their child's good, but his imagination was unpractised and would not help him much. He made one great effort for her sake. He took her abroad, and for a whole year travelled about, showing her much that was best worth seeing in the south of Europe - but seeing *places* chiefly, people seldom. In all this time she saw nothing of her cousin George - he had almost fallen out of her acquaintance, and taken the place of a disagreeable memory. But when she and her father came home, he was there to receive them, and she began to realize that his presence was to be an essential part of her home life. More than that, she now perceived how distinctly he stood between her and her father - a fact she had forgotten while they were together without him. The acquaintance and sympathy between them, which had been slowly growing up during their year of travel, froze to death now that he was there; and Mary, at eighteen, found herself completely isolated.

It did not occur to her father that she ought to go into society, or that she needed a chaperone. Society had lost all its charms for him; and he intended to marry his daughter early, and so give her the best of protection. Neither did it seem necessary to him that she should be consulted in any way about her marriage. However insubordinate she might as a child have been to others, to him, whenever they were brought into direct contact, she had always been perfectly submissive, and he expected her to continue so. To such a length had his confidence in the success of his plans gone, that he had never in any way hinted them to his daughter - the thing was settled, and had become a part of the course of nature, in no way requiring to be discussed. Under these circumstances, Mary spent two years of grown-up life at home. They were very wearisome and depressing years, partly from her position, partly from her strong, and always growing, dislike to the cousin, who was so much more to her father than she was. She saw very few people; now and then she went with her father to a dinner-party where most of the guests were "grave and reverend seigniors" like himself; now and then to a dance, where people were civil to her, and where some stranger in the neighbourhood would occasionally show signs of incipient admiration, pleasantly exciting to a girl in her teens. And now and then she had to receive visitors at home, feeling constrained and annoyed while she did so, by the invariable presence of George. There were neighbours who would gladly have been good to her. It was common for mothers to say to each other, "Poor Mary Wynter! I should like to ask here more, but I really dare not, Mr. Wynter is *so* odd," - and Mary had even a certain consciousness of this goodwill and its suppression; but there were other sayings, common as household words, among these same people, of which she had no suspicion. It would, perhaps, have changed the whole story of her life, if she had known that the reason why she lived as much apart from the whole region of lovemaking or flirtation as if she had been a staid matron of fifty, was the general belief that she was engaged, and before long to be married to the one man in the world whom she cordially hated. If she had known it then, she might, perhaps, have found a substitute for her cousin among her own equals and countrymen, but her entire unconsciousness, which they could not suspect, so deceived every possible lover as to make them believe her utterly out of their reach.

The only real enjoyment which brightened these dull years, came to Mary when she visited an old school-friend. There were two or three with whom she had kept up affectionate intercourse; and one, especially, whose house was her refuge whenever she could get permission to spend a week away from home. This girl had married at the very time of Mary's leaving school - she lived much in the world, and would have carried Mary into the whirl of dissipation if Mr. Wynter had allowed it. But he had restricted his daughter's visits to those times of the year when Helen Churchill and her husband were in the country, fatigued and glad of a few weeks of quiet; there Mary went to them, and found their quiet livelier than the liveliest of her home-life.

But in the spring of her twenty-first year, leave, often refused, was granted, and she joined the Churchills in London. The first week passed in a delightful confusion - whether her new dresses, or her unaccustomed liberty, or the opera, or the park, or the companionship of Helen, or the absence of George, were the most delightful, she would have been puzzled to say.

Mrs. Harry Coghill

The next week her head steadied a little - everything was delightful, but it was London, and not fairyland; it could not be denied that the rooms were hot, and that one came down rather tired in the morning. Mrs. Churchill, however, had a remedy for that. She had a pretty pair of ponies which carried her well out of London almost every morning, into fresh air and green lanes, and she took Mary with her. After breakfast they used to start, and make their expedition long or short, according to the day's engagements.

One morning they had completely escaped from town, and were driving along a pleasant road, shady and quiet, where, in those days, no suburban villas had sprung up, but where a park paling was overhung by trees on one side, and on the other, fields stretched away upon a gentle slope. They had lately met but few people, and Helen, never a very careful driver, had been letting her ponies do pretty much what they liked. At last the lively little animals, perhaps out of pure wilfulness, chose to take fright at something by the roadside; they made a sudden rush, and their mistress all at once found herself quite unable to hold them. There was no immediate danger, the road being both good and clear, but as they went on, their pace, instead of subsiding, seemed to increase. The carriage was not of the low build of these days, and the servant hesitated to risk a jump from his perch at the back. Meantime a corner was in sight, which it would be hazardous to turn at this pace. Mary sat, pale and terrified, only just sufficiently mistress of herself not to scream when suddenly, two men appeared coming towards them round the dreaded corner. In another moment the adventure was over - the ponies had been stopped by one of the two strangers, and were standing panting but subdued; and Helen, recovering her self-possession the moment she was out of danger, was leaning forward to pour out thanks and explanations.

Mary, having less to do, had more leisure to look at the new-comers. They were both young, and dressed like English gentlemen, but they had both something foreign and unusual in their appearance. But there was this difference - that the foreign aspect was of a kind singularly attractive in the one, and unattractive in the other. One might have been a Frenchman of *mauvais ton*, but that he spoke English like an American. The other, who resembled a very handsome Spaniard, spoke with a slight French accent, and in a remarkably musical voice. The handsome one, indeed, spoke very little - it was he who had first stepped into the road and caught the runaway ponies; but having done so, he left his companion to take the lead in replying to Mrs. Churchill's civilities. And when she finally begged to know their names, in order that her husband might also express his gratitude, it was the unprepossessing one who produced his card, and, having written an address upon it, gave it to her, saying that it would serve for both. He and his friend were fond of long walks, he added, neither of them being used to London life, and that was the cause of their being so fortunate as to have been of use to the ladies. He ended this little speech with an elaborate bow, his companion raised his hat, and they parted.

The ponies went home quietly enough, and Helen took care to look after her driving. She handed the card to Mary, who read on it, "Mr. Bailey," and an address, which Helen said was probably that of a lodging.

"I should like to know who the other is," she added; "he was very much the nicest looking. I must get my husband to call to-morrow, and then we shall know more about them."

Mary did not say much on the subject. Love at first sight may be fairly owned as a possibility, but it would be ridiculous to say that Mary Wynter had proved its reality. The thin end of the wedge, perhaps, had wounded her, and a succession of blows would easily drive it deep into her heart, or her fancy, as the case might be. Perhaps, too, it was more tempting to think of a stranger so attractive without being able to give him a name, than it would have been if he had to be recognized as Mr. Thomas Brown or Mr. John Robinson.

However that might be, she did not find her enjoyment of the day at all interfered with by the morning's incident. She and Helen paid some visits, then dined out, and finally arrived rather late at a house where there was a great evening gathering. This house was one at which she had not before been a guest, and she was full of lively curiosity about the people she was to meet there. The hostess was fond of collecting together all sorts of stray oddities, and of trying to further a scheme of universal brotherhood by mixing up in her drawing-room a most motley crowd, including all classes, from the ultra fine lady to the emancipated slave. It was not, perhaps, very amusing to the portion of her guests who found themselves lost in a sea of unknown faces, through which no pilot guided them; yet people went to her, partly because she was *grande dame*, and partly as to a lion show. Mrs. Churchill thought her country girl would be amused by one visit to this lady, and Mary was delighted at the prospect of seeing the possessors of various well-known names.

The rooms were very full when they arrived; and when, after considerable exercise of patience and perseverance, they had struggled in and got to a corner where they could breathe, and speak to each other, Helen said,

"Well, my dear, I hope you will find the sight worth the scramble - it is fuller than usual to-night, I think; and if I followed my own inclinations, I should try to slip round to a little room I know, where there are seldom many people, and rest there. But that would not be fair to you."

"Indeed it would," Mary answered. "Do let us go; we can perhaps move about a little, later, and I positively cannot breathe here now."

They worked their way accordingly to the little boudoir Helen spoke of. Their progress was not without incidents - now an acquaintance, now a celebrity, now a woolly-haired princess, now a jewelled Oriental, met them as they went; but at last they turned out of the crowd and passed into a room nearly dark, quite empty, and cool. "Nobody has found it out yet," said Helen, sinking into a chair with a sigh of relief.

They remained silent, enjoying the quiet and fresh air. A large window opening on a balcony occupied the greater part of one side of the room, and a glimmer of reflected light, and a murmur of voices, came from the windows of the great drawing-room which also opened to the balcony. But both light and sound were subdued to the pleasantest softness, and the night-air was still and sweet; Mary's seat was beside the window, Mrs. Churchill sat further back towards the middle of the room.

Presently there was a sound of steps on the balcony. Helen moved impatiently. "Somebody coming," she murmured.

Mary involuntarily raised her hand as a sign that she should be silent; a voice had begun to speak which she recognized with surprise. It was that of their acquaintance of the morning. He was speaking in French, with a bad accent, and a voice which sounded even more disagreeable than it had done when he spoke to Helen.

"Bah! one can breathe here. What a crowd! And, my good friend, allow me to remind you that you are not doing your duty. If you don't look a little more sharply after our interest we shall quarrel."

"What am I to do?" another voice answered, and this time the accent was perfect, and the tones marvellously harmonious. "You bring me here, into this horrible crowd, where I am stifled, and I do not see what I can do except answer everybody who speaks to me, and try to look as if I were not longing to get away."

"Do?" repeated the first. "Why, *pose* a little. I wish I had made you come in paint and feathers. I believe my lady would have liked it better."

They had been drawing nearer as they spoke, and now stepped

Mrs. Harry Coghill

into the room. Bailey, who was first, passed Mary without seeing her, but the gleam of Mrs. Churchill's dress caught his eye, and he paused abruptly.

Helen rose and moved a step towards him.

"Mr. Bailey," she said graciously, "you must allow me to introduce myself to you now that chance has given me the opportunity. I am Mrs. Churchill, and I am glad to be able to repeat my thanks for the service you did me this morning."

Upon this Bailey came forward; he had had time to make himself pretty certain that nothing serious could have been overheard, and was ready to receive with rather florid politeness all the acknowledgments and civilities offered.

Mary alone seemed to remember that the ponies had really been stopped, not by Bailey, but by the man who now stood silent near to her. She in turn rose, and spoke with some diffidence. "I should like to offer my thanks too. I think I was too frightened to say anything this morning, but indeed I thank you."

The stranger bowed. "You make too much of a very small matter," he answered; "the ponies would most likely have become quiet of themselves, only it did not seem certain they would have turned the corner quite safely."

"I am sure they would not; they were quite unmanageable, and we had not met anybody for a long time. That road is so quiet."

Mary went on talking, fascinated by the charm of the voice that replied to her, until other people did come in, and the spell was broken. But when Helen moved back into the larger rooms, and she was obliged to follow, she went dreamingly until they found themselves beside their hostess. Upon her Helen seized, and assailed her with questions. Who were these two men? But of all the amazing announcements Lady

Deermount had ever had to make respecting her guests, the most amazing perhaps was in her reply.

"He is an Indian Chief, your hero, a true, genuine Uncas, only educated; and the other is an American."

An Indian Chief! These were the days when Cooper's novels were the latest fashion, and many a girl's head was turned by visions of splendid heroes - stately, generous, brave, and beautiful - capable of everything that was grandest, noblest, and most fascinating. Here was one in *propria persona*; and one, too, who, in addition to all the heroic virtues, could speak excellent French and English, and dress like an English gentleman.

What wonder if that night mischief was done never to be undone, however long, however bitterly repented?

It would be too tedious to continue the story in detail. Lady Deermount had constituted herself the patroness of many adventurers, but never of one cleverer than Bailey. She absolutely believed and duly repeated the story he told her, which was briefly this: - His companion, whose many-syllabled Indian name he taught her, but who, in England, found his baptismal one of Christian more convenient, was the chief of a tribe once powerful, now fallen into decay. To raise this tribe again was his one idea, his fervent ambition. He had himself been educated by the French Jesuits, but, when fully informed, had seen the errors of their faith, and now earnestly desired to found among his people, English civilization and the Protestant religion. Money was needed; for this he had consented to come to England, accompanied by about a dozen men and women of his tribe, hoping that the sight of these poor creatures in all their native savagery would prevail upon the rich and generous to help him in his work of education.

What could be more interesting? As a matter of fact, considerable assemblies did gather, daily, to see the Indians perform their dances, or sing their songs, or to hear one of them relate their legends, which Christian translated into musical and fluent English. Bailey explained his own connection with the party by saying that they required some one to look after the more practical matters of lodging, food, etc., which Christian, a stranger in Europe, could not well do, and professed himself to be a mere hired accessory. It was Christian who was the soul of all, the hero, who, for a noble purpose, endured a daily mortification of his legitimate pride. And with Christian, Mary Wynter fell deeply in love. Everything helped her - nothing hindered. Did no other girl ever fall in love with a creature as purely of her imagination? A good many wives, perhaps, know something about it, and a good many old maids also - who are the better off.

When the visit to London ended, and she went back to the old solitary life, everything had changed to her. Her days, which had been empty, were full of dreams, her heart grew tender, glad, hopeful, with a sweet unreasonable content. Even George seemed less disagreeable to her; she began to think she had been often ill-tempered, and must try to make amends. Christian had found means - or Bailey had found them for him - to make her believe herself as much to him as he was to her. She knew that the whole party had left London, and were moving from place to place. By-and-by they would come to Cheshire, and then she would see or hear of them. Christian had not proposed to her to marry him, nor had she deliberately considered such a possibility - she loved him, and he would soon be near her again, that was enough for the present.

In this mood she passed the rest of summer, and the early autumn. Mr. Wynter and George spent most of the day together, and she saw little of them until dinner-time. The evenings were social, after a fashion. Sometimes Mary played or sung - sometimes George read aloud. Mr. Wynter liked to be amused, but he did not care to talk. Thus, even the hours they spent together led to no acquaintance between father and daughter - each was altogether in the dark as to the thoughts, feelings, and projects of the other.

One November morning Mary was sitting alone as usual. She had intended to go out, but it was grey and cheerless out of doors, and the attraction of a bright fire, and a new book, proved too strong for her. The book was one of her favourite Indian stories, and she lost herself in the delightful depths of the "forest primeval" with an entire and blissful forgetfulness of England and common sense. But she roused herself, with a start of no little surprise, when her father suddenly walked into the room.

"Papa!" she cried, jumping up and letting her book fall, with a sudden conviction that something important indeed, must have brought so unusual a visitor.

"Sit down, my dear," he answered kindly; "I have something to say to you. It did not seem necessary to say anything about it before, but now you are nearly twenty-one, and that is the time I have always fixed upon."

"Fixed upon for what, papa?" she said, utterly at a loss.

"For your marriage, my dear. It is a good age, quite young enough, and yet old enough for a girl to have some idea of her duties. I wish you to be married in February. A month after your birthday."

Mary looked at him in complete bewilderment. Her very marriage-day fixed, and where was the bridegroom? She almost laughed, as she thought that she could not even guess at any person who as likely to propose for her - except one.

"But who is it?" she managed to ask, at last. "Nobody wants to marry me."

"Who is it?" Mr. Wynter repeated in surprise. "George, of course."

"George!" she stopped a minute to recover breath.

Mr. Wynter remained silent. He had said all that was needful. She was going to say, "Papa, you must be joking," but she looked at his face and could not. He was too much in earnest - she perceived that with him the thing was settled - and therefore done. She took courage from the despair of the moment; "Papa," she said deliberately, "I will *never* marry my cousin George."

For one moment, his face seemed to change. Then he got up, as calm and assured as before.

"You are surprised, I see," he answered. "I supposed you must have guessed my intentions. I will speak with you about it again to-morrow."

So he went out, and left her stunned, but by no means beaten. And, from that day a struggle began - if indeed it could be called a struggle, where the one party had not the slightest comprehension of the resistance of the other. At Christmas, Mary, by this time driven almost frantic, heard of the arrival of Christian at Chester. They met by Bailey's contrivance, and Mary came back home pledged to marry her hero. Delay, however, was necessary. The marriage could not take place until just before the Indians sailed for Canada, which would be in March, and Mary could obtain delay, only by a kind of compromise. She made her cousin himself the means of obtaining this, by reminding him that the least he could do for her, was to give her time to reconcile herself to so new an idea. He, not the least in love, and far from suspecting a rival, asked that the marriage might be put off for three months. This was all that was needed. On the night of the 16th March, Mary left home, and travelled under Bailey's guidance to Liverpool. There Christian met her. All had been arranged, and they were married, and started for Ireland. After a week or two of honeymoon, they went to Queenstown, and there joined the ship, which was carrying the rest of the party to Quebec.

It was during the two or three weeks spent in Ireland, and still more completely during the voyage, that all the fair fabric of the young wife's delusions fell to pieces.

The truth of Bailey's history was very different from what he said of himself. He had been long the disgrace and torment of his own relations in the United States, and at last, after years of every kind of vice, had been obliged to fly from his country under strong suspicions of forgery. He went to the north, and for a year or two lived a wild life full of adventure; during which he occupied himself diligently in becoming acquainted with the Indian tribes, learning some of their dialects, and trying by every means to ingratiate himself with them. Probably at first, this was only for amusement, but after awhile, he seems to have entertained the idea of making a profit of his new associates. He soon found, however, that the more independent and uncivilized tribes, though they might form the most piquant exhibition, were too unmanageable for his purpose. He came down therefore to Canada, to seek for more promising materials. Here he met with exactly the opposite difficulty - most of the tribes were more or less civilized, and had, at any rate, advanced so far in knowledge of the world as to be unwilling to put themselves into his power. He soon saw that the best way of securing such a party as he wished, would be to find one Indian, whom he might make to some degree a confidant and partner in the enterprise, and who would naturally possess a stronger influence with the rest, than he could himself obtain. It was a long time before he succeeded in doing this; but when he did, it was to perfection. An island about fifty miles from Cacouna, called Moose Island, was then, and still is, occupied by a settlement of Ojibways. A Jesuit mission, established on the Canadian bank of the river, had been devoted to the conversion of these people, with so much success that nearly all of them were nominal Christians. For the rest, they lived in their own way, providing for themselves by hunting and fishing, and keeping their national customs and character almost unchanged. In the mission-house, however, a few children were brought up by the priests with the greatest care, - probably because it was by means of these boys, that they hoped more effectually to civilize the whole tribe. At any rate, they taught them all that they could have taught Europeans; having them completely in their own hands, there was no difficulty about this, and the more intelligent among them became good scholars. There was one boy, however, who distinguished himself above the rest, and was naturally the pride and favourite of the mission. He was an orphan, whom they had named Christian, and whom they were turning expressly for a priest. But when Christian was about sixteen, the mission was for the first time disturbed. Some Protestant missionaries invaded the island itself, and built their house close to the Indian wigwams. They spoke the language sufficiently to be understood, and took every means of making themselves acceptable to the people. They were men of great fervour and earnestness, and to the Indian senses, their religion, with its abundant hymns, and exclamatory prayers, had an attraction greater than that of the more decorous service to which they were accustomed. One by one, the so-called converts left the Jesuit church, and were re-converted with great acclamation. But when the infection reached their own pupils, their own particular and beloved flock, the priests were in despair; and the very first of their children to leave them, was Christian. He had been, for some time, tired of the sober and self-denying life which he was obliged to lead; and having gained all the advantages the priests could give him, and knowing that his profession of Protestantism would be hailed with the greatest joy by the new missionaries, he went to them, and so succeeded in persuading them of his sincerity, that he became as great a favourite as he had before been with his old teachers. The Jesuits, soon after, finding themselves almost entirely abandoned, gave up their mission and left the field to their opponents. How Christian spent the next few years it is not easy to tell. From the missionaries he learned to speak English perfectly well, and was for a time master of a school, which they established for the Indian children; but he lost their favour by the very same means by which he gained it. He was insincere in everything, and as he frequently visited both banks of the river, and was trusted to execute commissions for them, he had many opportunities for deceiving them. At last, he left the island altogether and joined a party of smugglers. With them he must have remained some time; but he had left them also and returned to the island, when Bailey came to the neighbourhood. They soon became acquainted; and Bailey, finding how exactly Christian suited his purpose, spared no pains to persuade him to join in collecting a sufficient number of his people for the expedition. In this he succeeded; but Christian was not to be imposed upon, and refused to stir in the matter, without an engagement from Bailey to pay him a considerable sum, on their return to Canada. Bailey was obliged to yield, and the agreement was signed, with a fixed determination to avoid keeping it, if possible. The other Indians were found without much trouble among those on the island, who, in spite of their change of teachers, were still in the same half-savage or more than half-savage state. A bad hunting season had reduced them to great misery, and a dozen of them were willing enough to undertake the voyage under the guidance of Christian, whose education had given him a kind of ascendancy to which he had no other claim, for the chieftainship, with which Bailey chose to invest him, was purely imaginary. Christian was a natural actor. Bailey understood perfectly what would suit the popular idea of an Indian chief, and the story which he intended to tell, so that, together, they succeeded admirably. They made a profitable tour, and their success culminated in London when they began to count leaders of fashion among their dupes.

It was at this moment of their success, that accident threw in their way a girl who was evidently well-born and susceptible, and whom a few inquiries proved to be an heiress. At first, Bailey had had some thought of himself winning this prize; but he had wit enough to see that he would not succeed, and that Christian might, which would be equally to his advantage. Christian cared little about it, but he let Bailey guide him, and so the prey fell into their hands.

So far, the story told had been intensely personal, and of the kind which must inevitably be coloured by the teller. From this point, Mrs. Costello was no longer leading her daughter through places and scenes entirely strange. She paused, and faltered, yet began again with a sense of having surmounted her greatest difficulties, and from hence is perhaps the best narrator of her own life.

"When I found out," she went on, "how different the reality was from my dreams, I took no care to hide, either from Bailey or my husband, the horror I began to feel for them both. Christian took my reproaches carelessly - his education had not prevented him from regarding women as other Indians do - to him I was merely his squaw, the chief and most useful of his possessions, and it made no difference to him whether I was contented with my position or not. But Bailey was not quite so insensible; and when I spoke to him with the same bitterness as to my husband, he retorted, and took trouble to show me how my own folly had been as much to blame as their schemes, in drawing me into such a marriage. He explained to me precisely how, and why, I had been entrapped, and made me perceive that I was utterly helpless in their hands. There came, about the middle of our voyage, a time when I sunk into a kind of stupor; worn out with the misery of my disappointment, I gave up my whole mind to a gloomy passiveness. Morning after morning I crept out on deck, and sat all day leaning against the bulwarks, with a cloak drawn round me, seeing nothing but the waves and sky, and indifferent to wind or rain, or the hot sun which sometimes shone on me. All this time I had taken no notice of the Indians, who for their part avoided me, and left me a portion of the deck always undisturbed. But one day as I sat as usual vacantly looking out to sea, I was disturbed by the cries of a child. The babies, although there were four or five in the party, were usually so quiet that the sound surprised me. I looked round, and saw the women gathered together in a group, consulting over the child, which still cried as if in violent pain. At last I got up, and went to the place, where I found that the poor little creature, a girl of about a year old, had fallen down a hatchway and broken her arm. She had lost her mother in England, and was in the care of an elder sister, who hung over her in the greatest distress, while the other women were preparing to bandage the arm. I had had no idea till then how wretchedly these poor creatures were huddled together, without even such comforts as they were used to; but when I found that it was impossible for the sick child to be cared for in the miserable place where they lived, I began to come to myself a little, or rather to forget myself, and contrive something to help others.

"The child's sister, Mary, spoke a little French, so that we could manage to understand each other; and with shawls and pillows, we made a comfortable little bed, in an unoccupied space close to my cabin. There we nursed the poor little creature, which got well wonderfully soon, and Mary became my firm and faithful friend. It was she whom you saw a few weeks ago, when she came, hoping to bring me a useful warning.

"We were six weeks at sea; and when we reached Quebec, and had to take the steamboats, a new kind of misery began for me. I shrank from the sight of our fellow-passengers, for I felt that wherever we went, they looked at me curiously, and sometimes I heard remarks and speculations, which seemed to carry the sense of degradation to my very heart. But Mary and her little sister had done me good. I had already lost some of my pride, and began to remember that, however I might repent my marriage, I had entered into it of my own will, and could not now free myself either from its ties or duties. My husband seemed pleased with my change of manner towards him; he was not unkind, and I hoped that perhaps when we reached his own tribe, and I had a home to care for, my life might not yet be so hopelessly wretched as it appeared at first.

"The last part of our journey was made in waggons. When we were within a few hours' distance of Moose Island the others went on, while Bailey, Christian, and I, remained at a small wayside tavern. It was a wretched place, but they gave me a small room where I could be alone, and try to rest. The one adjoining it was Bailey's, and late in the evening I heard him and Christian go into it together. The partition was so thin that their voices reached me quite distinctly, and I soon found that they were disputing about something. From the day

Mrs. Harry Coghill

when, on board ship, Bailey had told me how they had entrapped me simply for the money to which I was entitled, there had never been any allusion made, in my presence, to the profit they expected to make of me. I could hear now, however, as their voices grew louder, that this was the cause of their dispute. I caught only broken sentences, and never knew how the quarrel ended, for in the morning Bailey was gone, and I had learned already that it was useless to question Christian. I had written from Quebec to my father. The only answer I received was through his solicitor, who formally made over to me all my mother's fortune; but, of course, this did not happen until some weeks after our arrival at Moose Island.

"We remained three or four days at the tavern, and then removed to the island, where a small log-house had been got ready for me. It was clean and neat, though not better than the cottages of many farm-labourers in England, and I was so humbled that I never thought of complaining. It stood on a small marshy promontory at one end of the island, at a considerable distance from the village, and was more accessible by land than by water.

"In that house, Lucia, you were born; but not until three years of solitude, terror, and misery had almost broken my heart.

"As soon as ever we were settled in our home, which I tried to make comfortable and inviting according to my English ideas, Christian returned to the wandering and dissipated life he had led in the last few years before his journey to England. He was often away from me for many days without my knowing where he was, and I only heard from others, vague stories of his spending nights and days, drinking and gambling, on the American side of the river. At first, he always came back sober, and in good humour, and never left me without sufficient money for the few expenses which were necessary; but within six months this changed, and I began to suffer, not only from ill-usage, but from want.

"The missionaries, of whom I told you, were still on the island when I arrived there; but although they pitied, and were disposed to be kind to me, I could not bear to complain to them, or to make my story a subject for missionary reports and speeches. You see I had a little pride still, but I do not know whether it would not have yielded to the dreadful need for a friend of my own race, if events had not brought me one whom you know, Mr. Strafford.

"Although the island was large enough to have maintained the whole Indian population by farming, it remained, when I came there, entirely uncultivated, and hunting and fishing were still the only means the people had of supporting themselves. The consequence was, that at times they suffered greatly from scarcity of provisions, and this naturally brought disease. The year after my marriage was a bad one, and the women and children especially felt the want of their usual supplies. A great many of them left the island, and tried to find food by begging, or by selling mats, and baskets, at the nearest settlements. The misery of these poor creatures attracted attention, and people began to wonder why, since they were Christians, and had received some degree of teaching, they were still so ignorant of the means of living. The answer was easy. The missionaries who had taught them were as ignorant as themselves of these things; and, indeed, had not thought it necessary to civilize while they Christianized them. Mr. Strafford had then lately arrived in the country. He held different views to those of the missionaries, and, pitying the forlorn condition of the islanders, he offered to come and help them. Almost the first sensation of gladness I remember feeling, from the day I left my father's house, was when I heard that a clergyman of our own Church was to be settled among my poor neighbours."

Mrs. Harry Coghill

CHAPTER X

"Mr. Strafford had been some little time on the island before he saw me. I had seen him, however, and I dare say you will understand how the expression of his face, the honest, manly, kindly look you have often admired, filled me with indescribable consolation, for I felt that there would be near me, in future, a countryman on whose counsel and help I could rely, if I should be driven to extremity. I waited without any impatience for the visit which he was sure to pay me. Mary, my best friend, had lately married a young Indian, who had spent much of his life among Europeans, and who was now employed by Mr. Strafford to teach him the Ojibway language, and, in the meantime, to act as interpreter for him. Through Mary and her husband, Henry Wanita, I knew he would hear of me and be sure to seek me out. I was right; he came one day when I was, as usual, alone, and before he left I had told him as much of my story as I could tell to any one, except to you. I expected that he would pity me, and that his pity would have a little contempt mixed with it, and I had made up my mind to endure the bitterness of this, for the sake of establishing that claim upon his advice and aid, which I was certain, after the first shock of such a confession, my wretchedness would give me. But he had not one word of reproof to say; either he had heard, or he guessed that my fault had brought its full measure of punishment, and that what I needed was rather consolation than reproach. He went away and left me, as he often left me afterwards, with courage and patience renewed for the hard struggle of my life.

"My husband had lately been more than ever away; and though in his absence I had often the greatest difficulty to obtain food, or any kind of necessaries, yet I was thankful for the peace in which I could then live. I learned to embroider in the Indian fashion, and was able to repay the kindness I received from Mary, and some of the other squaws, by drawing patterns for them, and by teaching them how to make more comfortable clothes for themselves and their children. After Mr. Strafford had been a little while on the island, he proposed to establish a school for this kind of work, and I became the mistress. The women and girls came to me more readily than they would have done to a stranger, and I soon had a good number of pupils.

"Several months passed, after Mr. Strafford's coming, without anything new occurring. Then Christian returned from the States, where he had been for a longer time than usual. He came late at night, and so intoxicated that I was obliged to go myself and fasten the canoe, which would have floated away before morning. When I followed him into the house he was already fast asleep, and it was not till the next day that I knew what had brought him home. Then he told me. What I understood - for he said as little as possible on the subject - was, that he had been for the last few weeks in the company of a party of gamblers, to whom he had lost everything he possessed, and, finally, that having found means of raising money upon the security of the whole fortune to which I was entitled, he had lost that too, and consequently we remained penniless. This much I heard with indifference; the money he received had never benefited me, and had only given him the means for a life you cannot imagine, and which I could not, if I would, describe to you; but when he ended by telling me that, as all my relations were rich, I must contrive to get fresh supplies from some of them, my patience gave way altogether. Even my fear of him yielded to my anger; for the first time since our arrival in Canada I spoke to him with all the bitterness I felt. A horrible scene followed - he threatened to kill me, and I believe would have done it but for the hope of yet obtaining money by my means. I tried to escape, but could not; and, at last, when he was tired of torturing me, he took off a long red sash which he wore, and tied me to the bed. There, Lucia, for four-and-twenty hours he kept me a prisoner, standing in a constrained attitude, without rest or food. How I endured so long without fainting, I do not know; fear of something worse must have given me unnatural strength, for he never left the house, but spent the early part of the day in searching all my cupboards and boxes for money or anything worth money, and the later part in drinking. Mr. Strafford had gone over to the Canadian shore, or probably, missing me from the school, he would have come in search of me. Mary did come, but at the sight of my husband, she went away without knowing anything of me. All night he sat drinking, for he had brought a quantity of whisky home some time before, and towards morning he lay down for a while, but so that I could not move without disturbing him. After two or three hours' sleep he got up and went away, leaving me still tied, and telling me I had better think of what he had said, and make up my mind to get money in some way. When I heard the sound of his paddle, and knew that he was really gone, the force that had sustained me gave way; I fainted, and in falling, the sash happily broke, though not until one of my wrists was badly sprained. The pain of my wrist brought me back to consciousness. As soon as I could, I wrapped myself in a shawl and went to Mary's cottage, to ask her to bandage it for me, and to take my excuses to the school, where I was quite unable to go that day.

"No one, not even Mr. Strafford, knew the cause of my sprained wrist, or the conduct of my husband that day and night, but it was impossible that when such scenes were repeated again and again, they should not become known. And they were repeated so often and so dreadfully, that only the feeling that I endured the just penalty of my own conduct, enabled me to bear the perpetual suffering. At last, even Christian saw that I could not live long if I had not some respite. Perhaps he had a little pity for me; perhaps he only thought still of gain. At any rate, he became less cruel, and my health returned. Again something like a calm came over my life, and I began to feel hopeful once more. The next spring you, Lucia, my light and comfort, were born, and from that time I had double cause both for hope and fear. The birth of a daughter, however, is no cause of joy to an Indian father; if you had been a boy you would have been (or so I fancy) far less consolation to me, but to Christian you would have been more welcome. He was with me when you were born, but the very next day he left the island for three or four weeks, and from the time of his next return all my former sufferings recommenced. Often in terror for your life, I carried you to Mary Wanita and implored her to keep you until your father was gone; and even in his absence I scarcely dared to fall asleep with you in my arms, lest he should come in unexpectedly and snatch you from me.

"When you were about a year old Mr. Strafford married. His wife, who had already heard of me before her marriage, became the dearest of friends to me; with her I could always leave you in safety, and with her I began to feel again the solace of female society and sympathy. She is dead, as you know, long ago, and her little daughter died at the same time, of a fever which broke out on the island two or three years after we left it.

"Two years passed after your birth, and things had gone on in much the same way. My husband never ceased to urge me to try to obtain money from England, and in the meantime he continually took from me the little I could earn by my work, for which Mrs. Strafford found me a sale in different towns of the province.

"Do not misjudge me, Lucia. I tell you these things only to justify what I did later, and my long concealment even from you of the truth of my history.

"But when you were about two years old your father left the island, and did not return. The longest stay he had ever made before was a month, and when two passed, and I neither saw nor heard of him, I began to feel uneasy. Mr. Strafford made many inquiries for me, but we only heard of his having been seen shortly after he left home, and quite failed in learning where he had gone. Time went on, and, after the first anxious and troubled feelings passed off, I allowed myself to enjoy the undisturbed quiet, and to be happy as any other mother might be with her child. I had a whole year of such peace; you grew hardy and merry, and were the pet and plaything of the whole village, learning to talk the strangest mixed language, and showing at that time none of the terror of Indians which I have seen in you since then.

"But at the end of a year our respite ended. One day when I had been at the school, and you with me, I was surprised on my return home to see the door of the house open, and some men sitting at my table. I hurried on, and walked into the room before they were aware of my coming. There were four of them, two Indians and two who were either white or of mixed race; but it was only by his voice, and that after a moment's pause, that I could recognize my husband. My husband! never till then had I known the full horror that word could convey. Remember that long ago I had been charmed, had fallen in love, as girls say, with one who seemed to represent the very perfection and ideal of manly beauty; that this beauty and stateliness of outward form had been so great that I took it for the truthful expression of such a nature as I thought most heroic - remember this, and then think of what I saw after this year of absence. A bloated, degraded, horrible creature - not even a man, but a brute, raving half deliriously, and still drinking, while his companions, little more sober than himself, made him the subject of their jests and jeers. I held my little innocent child in my arms while I saw this, and for the first time, and for her sake, I felt a bitter hatred rise up in my heart against her father."

A strong shudder crept over Mrs. Costello; she covered her face with her hands for a moment, while Lucia drew more closely to her side. Presently she went on. "A cry from you, my child, drew the men's attention to us. 'Here's your squaw,' one of them said to Christian, who tried to get up, but could not. I saw that it was useless to speak to him, and turned to leave the house, intending to ask shelter from Mrs. Strafford or Mary, but before I could pass the door one of the strangers shut and bolted it, while another seized and held me fast. They made me sit down at the table; they tried to drag you out of my arms, and failing in that, to make you swallow some of the whisky they were drinking. I defended you as well as I could. In my terror and despair I watched for the time when they should all become as helpless as the miserable creature who had brought them there; but it was long to wait. Lucia, those hours when I saw myself and you at the mercy of these wretches were like years of agony. They saw my fear, however I might try to disguise it, and delighted in the torment I suffered. They tried again and again to take you from me; they threatened us both with every imaginable horror; till I thought night would have quite closed in before their drinking would end in complete intoxication. At length, at length, it did. One had fallen asleep; the other two were quarrelling feebly, when I ventured to move. They tried to get up, to stop me; but I drew the bolt, and fled into the darkness where I knew they could not follow.

"I reached Mr. Strafford's door, and we were received with all kindness; but the fright, the sudden exposure to cold night air, after being for so many hours shut up in a stifling room, and perhaps, added to all a few drops of spirit which had been forced into your mouth, brought on you a sudden, and to me most terrible, illness. It was your first; I had never seen you suffer, and I thought you would die; that God would take you from me as the last and crowning punishment for my disobedience. In the great anguish of this idea, I wrote to my father - wrote by your bedside while you slept, and confessing all my folly, implored his forgiveness, as if that would preserve my child's life. You recovered, and in my joy I almost forgot that the letter had been written. While you lay ill, the Straffords concealed from me that my husband had been to the house demanding my return home; but when you were almost well, they told me not only this, but that he had declared in the village that he would punish us both for our flight. It was then that Mr. Strafford recommended me to think seriously of a final escape.

"'It is evident,' he said, 'that you neither can, nor ought, to put yourself and your child again into his power - while you remain on the island it must be here; but I strongly advise you to return to England, or conceal yourself from him in some way.'

"I gratefully accepted his invitation to remain for a little while at his house - the rest of his plan could not be hastily decided upon; and while I deliberated, a letter arrived from England. Mr. Strafford, on hearing of the scene which ended in your illness, had carried out an idea which, he afterwards told me, he had long entertained, and written to my cousin George. The letter which now arrived was in answer to this, though it contained an enclosure for me. My appeal to my father had been made just in time; it reached him on his deathbed, and he forgave me. He did more than that; he altered, at the very last, a will made many years before, and left me an equal sum to that I had before inherited from my mother, but with the condition that I should never return to England. You understand now why, loving the dear old country as I still do, I have always told you I should never see it again - to do so would be to forfeit all our living, and more even than that, it would be to disobey my father's last command. My cousin's note was as kind and brotherly as if he had never had the least reason to complain of me. He told me that he had married some years before a good woman who, I have since thought, might have been his first choice if regard for my father's wishes had not influenced him. At any rate, they were and, I hope, still are happy together, filling my father and mother's places in the old home.

"These letters made my way clearer. It was settled that I should take advantage of Christian's absence (for he had again left the island) to remove with you to the most secure hiding-place we could find, and as a large town always offers the best means of concealment, we decided upon Montreal. So after a residence of six years on the island, I left it at last, carrying you with me and calling myself a widow. It was then that I took the name of Costello. It was my mother's family name, and is really, as you have always supposed, Spanish - my great-grandfather having been a Spaniard. I gave you the name at your baptism, so that it is really yours, though not mine.

"For six months we remained in Montreal; but I had been so long used to the silence and free air of the island that my health failed in the noisy town. I was seized with a terror of dying, and leaving you unprotected, and therefore determined to try whether I could not remain concealed equally well in the country. A chance made me think of this neighbourhood, which, though rather too near my old home, was then very retired, and not inhabited at all by Indians. I came up, found this place for sale and bought it. There was only a very rough log-house upon the ground, but I went into that until this cottage was ready, and here you can remember almost all that has happened."

Lucia raised her head as her mother finished speaking.

"But - my father!" she said hesitatingly.

"I forgot." Mrs. Costello resumed. "Mr. Strafford kept me informed of his movements for some time. He came back shortly after we had left the island, and on finding us gone, he tried all means to discover where we were. He actually traced us to Montreal, but there lost the clue, and came back disappointed. For some years he continued to live much as he had done ever since his return from England, frequently staying two or three weeks on the island, and never forgetting to make some effort to trace us. The perpetual terror I suffered during those years never subsided. I feared to go outside of my own garden lest he should meet and recognize me. At last Mr. Strafford sent me word that he had gone to the Hudson's Bay Territory.

"After that I began to feel that I was free, and from the time you were nine until you were sixteen I had little immediate anxiety; then, as I saw you growing up, I knew that the time when you must know your own birth and my history drew very near, and the idea weighed on me constantly. Other anxieties came too, and finally, worst of all, news that Christian had returned."

"And now," Lucia asked, "do you know where he is?"

"No. But I have been warned that he is seeking for us. They say that we have more reason than ever to fear him, and that he is looking for us in this part of the province."

Mrs. Costello's voice sunk almost to a whisper. She seemed to fancy that the man she had so long escaped might be close at hand, and Lucia caught the infection of her terror. They remained silent a minute, listening fearfully to the light rustling of the leaves outside, as the breeze stirred them.

"Mother," Lucia said at last, "how soon can we leave here?"

"I have thought much of that," Mrs. Costello answered, "but we have ties here too strong to be broken suddenly; and, indeed, a hasty removal might but draw upon us the very notice we wish to avoid."

"We must go soon though, as soon as possible. Oh! mamma, I could not bear to stay here now."

It was a cry of impatience - of acute pain - the child had suddenly turned back from her mother's story to her own trial and loss. Love, happiness, two hours ago clasped to her heart, and now torn from her pitilessly; for a moment she was all rebellion at the thought - she, at least, had not sinned, why should she suffer? Yet in her heart she knew that she must; she saw the one path clear before her, and felt that the time for acting was now; the time for grieving must come after. She rose, and walked up and down the room, gathering her strength and courage as she could.

At last she stopped in front of her mother's chair. Her face was pale, but so steady and composed that its girlishness seemed gone - she looked, what she would be from that time, a woman able to endure, and resolute to act.

"Mother," she said quietly, "Mr. Percy is coming to-morrow morning. He is coming to see you, but I would rather speak to him myself. There is no need that he should know anything whatever - of my father, or of what you have told me - we shall never see him again."

Except once, there was neither hesitation nor faltering in her voice, but her meaning could not be misunderstood. For a moment Mrs. Costello felt her convictions and her judgment shaken; if, after all, this love, which Lucia was about to lose, should be true and perfect? if Percy should be capable of knowing all, and yet cherishing and prizing her? Ought pride, ought her own opinion of him, to stand between her child and possible happiness and safety?

But she saw in Lucia's face that underneath all her love, the same feeling, that his would not stand this shock, lay deep in her heart, and the doubt died away as suddenly as it had risen.

"Do as you will, my child," she said. "But think well first. I, who have failed where I most desired to succeed, cannot venture now to advise you."

Lucia bent down and kissed her. "Poor mother!" she said tenderly, "you have thought too much for me, and I have never known what a burden I was to you. But we shall do better in future - when we are far away and have begun life again."

The hopeful words sounded very dreary in the sweet young voice, which seemed to have changed its tone, and taken the low mournful intonation of her Indian race; but she moved calmly away, replaced the contents of the desk with care, and closed and locked it. Then she gave the key to her mother, and

Mrs. Harry Coghill

bent over her again to say good-night.

There were no more words spoken between them. A long kiss, and they separated. But for the first time Mrs. Costello did not visit her daughter's room - she guessed that a battle had to be fought there in solitude, and that hers was not the only vigil kept that night. So the two watched apart; and the dawn, which was not far distant when they bade each other good-night, came in and found them both looking out with sleepless eyes at the grey sky and the familiar landscape, from which they were each planning to escape for ever.

But as the sky reddened, Lucia remembered that her sleepless night would leave traces which she wished to avoid, in her pale cheeks and heavy eyes. She lay down therefore, and at last fell asleep. Her over-excited brain, however, could not rest; the most troubled and fantastic dreams came to her, - her mother, Mary Wanita, Percy, Maurice, and many other persons seemed to surround her - but in every change of scene there appeared the shadowy figure of her father, constantly working or threatening harm. Sometimes she saw him as he looked in his portrait, and shrank from him as a kind of evil genius, beautiful and yet terrible - sometimes like the Indian who had met her by the river, a hideous, scarcely human object. Then, last of all, she saw him distinctly, as the scene her mother had described, the last time when she had really seen him, came before her, not by the power of imagination but of memory. For, waking up, she knew that, impressed upon her childish recollection by terror, that scene had never been entirely forgotten. Having no clue to its reality, she had always supposed it to be a dream; but now as it came back with some degree of vividness, she saw plainly the face which was neither that of the likeness nor that of her assailant, but might well be a link between the two - the same face in transition.

The idea was too horrible. She rose, and tried by hurried dressing to drive it from her mind; but it returned persistently. She went, at last, to her looking-glass and looked into it with a terror of herself. Never was ugliness so hateful as the beauty she saw there. For there could be no doubt about this, at least; except for the softening into womanly traits, and for a slightly fairer complexion, the picture her glass showed her was a faithful copy of that other, which she had seen for the first time last night. What beauty her mother had ever possessed had been thoroughly English in its character - hers was wholly Indian. She turned away with a feeling of loathing for herself, and a fearful glance into her heart as if to seek there also for some proof of this hateful birthright.

CHAPTER XI

When Mr. Percy left Lucia standing at the gate, and began his solitary walk back to Cacouna, he was almost as happy as she was. A kind of intoxication had swept away out of his very recollection the selfishness and policy of his habitual humour, - all that was youthful, generous, and impulsive in him had sprung suddenly to the surface, and so for the moment transformed him, that he was literally a different man to what he had ever been before. He pictured to himself the lovely bright face of the young girl as his daily companion - a Utopian vision of a small home where he was to be content with her society, and she with his, and where by some magic or other everything was to be arranged for them with an elegant simplicity which he, for that moment, forgot would be expensive to maintain, rose before his eyes; and he had almost reached his cousin's house, before this extraordinary hallucination began to yield a little, and his dreams to be interspersed with recollections of an empty purse and an angry father.

Alas! the wife and the home were but visions - the empty purse and the angry father were realities. That very morning a letter from the Earl had brought him a severe lecture on the folly of his delay in Canada; there was a sharp passage in it too about Lady Adeliza, who seemed to be in danger of deserting her truant admirer for one more assiduous. But indeed it was useless to think of Lady Adeliza now, for whatever might happen he was pledged to Lucia, and it would be well if her ladyship did really relieve him by accepting somebody else. Whether she did or no, however, he felt that his conduct towards her would furnish his father with sufficient cause for a quarrel, even without the added enormity of presenting to him a penniless daughter-in-law, who had not even family influence for a dower.

Poor Mr. Percy! he went into the house in grievous perplexity. Very much in love, more so than anybody, even himself, would have supposed possible, but very much doubting already whether the doings of the last hour or two had not been of a suicidal character, he tried to solve his difficulties by laying the whole blame upon fate. But to blame fate is not enough to repair the mischief she may have done; and though he succeeded in putting off his anxieties, so as not to let them be evident during the remainder of the evening, they returned with double force as soon as he was alone.

Mr. Percy naturally hated thinking; he hated trouble, and it was troublesome to think. Perhaps it was more troublesome to him than to other people; for, to confess the truth, he had not more than a very ordinary allowance of brains, and those he had were not accustomed to have sudden calls upon them. So he sat and pondered slowly, starting from the one or two points which were clear to him, and trying, without much success, to make out a map of the future from these slight indications. First of all, if was clear and evident that he was engaged to Lucia; he stopped a moment there to think of her, and that she was certainly a prize in the lottery of life, so beautiful, gracious, and devoted to him as she was; but he had not the smallest uncertainty about Mrs. Costello's consent, so never glanced towards any possible missing of the prize. That was all very well, *very* well, at present, though undeniably it would have been better if Lucia could have had Lady Adeliza's advantages. Ah! that was the next step. There was Lady Adeliza to be got rid of - if she did not herself, take the initiative - and that was not a pleasant affair. He had only been extremely attentive to her, that was the utmost anybody could say; but then there was his father - the two fathers, indeed, for he had good reason to believe that the Earl had not urged him to pay his suit to the lady without pretty good cause for counting on the approval of her family. It was a dreadful bore; and then there could be no doubt that by displeasing at a blow his own father and Lady Adeliza's, he was forfeiting his best if not his only chance of success in life. Altogether, the more he looked at the prospect the gloomier it grew, and at last he got up impatiently and put an end to his cogitations.

"I shall have to turn backwoodsman at once," he said to himself, "or miner, like those fellows we saw at the Sault."

In spite of his confidence in himself and in Lucia, it was not without a little tremor that Mr. Percy walked up to the Cottage next morning. He began to feel that there really might be some difficulty in persuading a mother to give up her only child to the care of a man who was not only poor, but likely to remain so, who could not even give her the hope of independence such as might fall to the lot of the backwoodsman or miner. But he kept up his courage as well as he could, and was very little disturbed out of his usual manner when he followed Margery into the small parlour. The room was empty; and in a little surprise - for he expected Lucia would have prepared her mother for his coming - he walked to the window and looked out on to the verandah. There was no one there, nor in the garden, but the sound of a door opening made him turn round, as Lucia, instead of Mrs. Costello, came in.

As they met he saw a change in her. A crimson colour had rushed to her face for a moment when she came in, but in a moment faded to the most complete pallor. There was not a sign of her usual shy grace or timid welcome: she was cold, erect, and composed, nothing more.

She gave him her hand, and said,

"My mother is not well. I must speak to you for her, Mr. Percy, and for myself."

"But Lucia!" he cried. "What is this? What is the matter? Have you forgotten last night?"

Her quiet was shaken for a moment.

"No, indeed," she answered. "No. I shall never forget last night."

"You have surely forgotten what I came for this morning then," he said placing a chair for her. "Sit down and tell me what is wrong, for something is." His tone, his look, so utterly unsuspicious of anything that could come between them in this trouble of hers, were hard to bear. But she had to speak.

"Something is wrong at present," she said steadily; "but we can set it right. I made a terrible mistake last night. You must go away and forget all we said to each other."

He looked at her incredulously.

"Explain," he said.

She had to pause for a moment. If it were but over!

"Pray believe what I say," she answered, forming the words slowly and with difficulty. "I found out last night after you had gone away that it was a mistake and a wrong - that you could not marry me, nor I you. Do you understand?"

"No, by heaven!" he cried. "If this is a jest - but it does not look like one. Did you mean what you said last night?"

"Yes, yes. I meant it then. See, I am a true woman. I have changed my mind already."

There was a bitter tone of jesting now, for she caught at any means of keeping down the sobs which would rise in her throat. He took her hand in a hard grasp.

"Look at me honestly and say what you mean; I am neither to be offended nor made a fool of. I want to know why you make a promise one day and try to break it the next?"

She looked at him for a moment, and then let her eyes fall with a heavy sigh.

"I hoped you would have been satisfied," she said, "to know that our engagement is broken; but it is true, you have a right to know more. I told you last night that I had no fortune. To-day I tell you that I have a portion you would never endure to receive with your wife, and which no man shall receive with me - disgrace."

She covered her face with her hands as she said the last word, and he could see nevertheless how the hot flush of shame rose to her forehead. He started, and involuntarily moved a step away from her. She was conscious of the movement, and raised her head proudly.

"How or in what way I should disgrace you," she went on, "I need not tell you - it is enough that you are satisfied that there is a bar between us." But he had recovered from his first surprise, and was in no mood to be so easily satisfied.

"You are mistaken," he said. "Disgrace is a terrible word; but how do I know that you are not frightening yourself and me with a shadow? Be reasonable, Lucia; you are suffering, I can see. Put aside this manner, which is so unlike yourself, and tell me what troubles you, and let me judge."

"Oh, if I could!" she cried, with a passionate longing breaking through all her self-restraint. She was trembling with excitement and the strain upon her nerves; and as she felt his arm put round her, it seemed for one second incredible that she must put its support away from her for ever. But she conquered herself, and spoke more resolutely than before.

"It is no shadow that I fear, but a calamity which has fallen upon us. I thought yesterday that I was not very far beneath you in birth, and that there could be no greater difficulties in our way than patience might overcome; but that was because I did not know. I am not your equal. I am no one's equal in the world - no one's that I could marry. I shall be always alone, and apart from other people in my heart, however they may see no difference; and if I cared for you a thousand times more than I do, I should only have a thousand more reasons for telling you to go away, and never think of me again."

"You dismiss me, then? Of your own free will, Lucia?"

"Of my own free will."

"And you will not tell me this strange secret which has changed you so?"

"No; there is no need."

"No need truly, if we are to part in this way. But you see that there is something romantic and unreal about the whole thing. I don't yet understand."

"No; how should you?" she said, half to herself. "I hardly can myself."

"Let me see your mother. I will come again, though my time is short."

"You need not. Mamma approves of what I say. Indeed, I cannot bear any more. Let me go. Good-bye."

She was growing of a more deathly paleness every moment, and the hand she offered him was cold as ice.

"Good-bye, then," he replied. "I am to consider all the past as a pleasant dream, am I?"

She raised her heavy, aching eyes to his face. His reproaches, if he had any to make, died away before that look, which betrayed endurance, taxed to the utmost - a burden on her own heart far heavier than that she laid on his. He held her hand for a moment.

"I don't understand," he repeated; "but I can't give you up so readily. Think over all this again, and if you find that you have decided too hastily, send me one line to say so; but it must be to-day. If I hear nothing from you, I shall leave Cacouna to-morrow."

"Yes," she answered passively. "Good-bye."

"Good-bye."

She stood without moving until the sound of the gate assured her that he was gone; then she sank down on the floor, not fainting nor weeping, but utterly exhausted. There her mother found her in a strange, heavy stupor, beyond tears or thought, and lifted her up, and made her lie down on her bed, where she fell into a heavy sleep, and woke in a new world, where everything seemed cold and dark, because hope and love had left her when she entered it.

Mr. Percy went back to Cacouna in greater perplexity than he had left it; nay, not merely in perplexity, but in real pain and mortification. If he had not seen plainly that Lucia was suffering bitterly, he would have been much more angry and less sorry; but, as it was, the whole thing was a mystery. Somehow he was very slow to believe that disgrace - any disgrace he could comprehend - really attached to her; his first idea, that she was making a great matter out of some trifle or mistake, had not yet left him, and he wished heartily that he could get at the truth, and see whether it was the insuperable obstacle she fancied it. He thought Mrs. Bellairs might help him in solving the question. He knew quite well that she was not particularly pleased with his attentions to Lucia, but she was both sensible and kind-hearted, and, when she knew how far matters had gone, he did not doubt that she would do what she could to save them both from a painful misunderstanding. But no sooner had he quickened his steps with the idea of immediately seeking her advice, than he began to reflect that Lucia had said she herself had been ignorant of any reason for acting as she had just done until last night; it was, therefore, very unlikely that Mrs. Bellairs, dear friend though she was, knew anything of this matter. And if there was a family secret, what right had he to betray it?

He gave up, therefore, this hope, and tried to content himself with the other, on which, however, he placed little reliance, that Lucia herself might recall him before the day was over. In the almost certainty that he had lost her, it was strange how completely he again forgot the difficulties that had troubled him before, and thought simply of her. At that moment he would willingly have sacrificed everything he *could* sacrifice for the knowledge that her secret was only a phantom, and that she was really to be his wife. Of course such a mood could not last. As evening drew on, and there was no word or sign from the Cottage, he began to feel angry both with Lucia and himself; and at night, when he had announced to his host and hostess that he should leave them by the next day's boat, he had made another step, and begun to think it possible that this state of affairs was better and more sensible than if he had been successful in his plan for delaying his journey a little longer and taking a bride home with him. After all, he concluded, this might only be a delay. If Lucia had refused to marry him, she had also declared that she would not marry at all. She meant, therefore, to remain free, and a year hence perhaps all might yet come right. If she cared for him, she would have come to her senses by that time, and be more able to judge whether they really must remain apart or not.

But early in the morning, when he woke, and remembered that it was the last time he would wake in her neighbourhood, he was seized with an unconquerable longing to see her again, however fruitlessly. He stole out softly, and walked to the Cottage. He knew that Lucia often worked among her flowers early, and guessed that that morning she would not be likely to sleep. He looked eagerly into the garden. She was not there, but he caught the flutter of her dress on the verandah; and thus encouraged, he walked to the door boldly and knocked; but Lucia had seen him also. She hurried to her own room. And when Margery, much amazed, came to tell her that Mr. Percy was asking for her, she said quietly, "Tell him that I have not left my room yet, and that I wish him a safe and prosperous voyage." They were the first words she thought of, and they sufficed. He went home, and commenced his preparations for departure without further delay; by that means greatly contenting Mrs. Bellairs, who at present wished for nothing so much as to be rid of her handsome guest. She was very civil to him, however, in the prospect of his going away, and the temptation to speak to her about Lucia again beset him strongly. But then to tell her, or even hint to her ever so slightly, that he had been rejected by a little simple Canadian girl, was not so easy a matter to his masculine pride as it would have been yesterday, so the time passed, and nothing was said.

As the boat went down the river Mr. Percy stood on deck, and watched anxiously for the Cottage, hoping to catch the flutter of a light dress, and to know that Lucia saw him go. But all was still and seemingly deserted; not a sign of her presence was visible, though he strained his eyes to the last moment. Yet she was watching also. Wrapped in a dark cloak, she stood among the trees, where she knew the shadows would conceal her, and took that last look which she had not courage to forbid herself. She put her arm round the slender trunk of an acacia tree, and, leaning forward, followed the receding boat, with a sickening eagerness, till it had completely disappeared; then her head sank for a moment against the tree, with one bitter yet suppressed cry. Sorrow was so new to her yet.

Little had been said between the mother and daughter in this crisis of Lucia's life. Mrs. Costello watched her child's pale and exhausted looks with painful solicitude, but she knew that words were useless. There was, therefore, neither complaint nor condolence; they went on with their usual occupations, and spoke, though not much, of their usual subjects. One thing, certainly, was different. Mrs. Costello went, instead of Lucia, to pay the long daily visit to Mr. Leigh. She said she wanted herself to have a consultation with him, about some small affairs in which she had been used to consult him, and Lucia was thankful to be spared, for one day, the danger of her old friend's scrutiny. But on the next day she went herself. A note from Mr. Strafford had reached them, accounting for his delay, and saying that he would arrive that evening, the very evening of Mr. Percy's departure, and she wished to go with her new self into more familiar company before facing one who, though so closely connected with the secret of her life, was almost a stranger to her.

She took with her a new book, and contrived as soon as possible to read instead of talking. It required less effort, and while she read, her mind could go back to the thoughts which were still in the stir and commotion of their recent disturbance. But all her efforts could not bring back to her face and voice the natural joyousness which had died out of them. A stranger would have seen no signs of emotion or trouble in her look and manner, but this was the utmost she could accomplish. To familiar, and above all, to loving eyes, the change was as evident as it was sorrowful; and Mr. Leigh speculated much on the subject. Guessing more truly than perhaps others of her associates might do, he wrote to Maurice that night that he feared some heavy trouble either threatened, or had come upon Mrs. Costello and Lucia. The same evening Mr. Strafford came to the Cottage. It was a year since his last visit, and the events which had taken place in the meantime made him even more than usually welcome to Mrs. Costello. He scarcely needed to be told that Lucia had now, at last, heard the story of her birth - he read it in her face, and rejoiced that there was full confidence between mother and daughter. As the three sat together round the fire - for the evenings were already growing chilly, and the leaves in the garden began to fall - they spoke together of the subject on which Mrs. Costello had been so anxiously waiting her friend's counsel.

"I am afraid you are right," Mr. Strafford said. "The only way to avoid, with certainty, any danger of meeting, is for you to leave Canada."

"It is hard for both of us," Mrs. Costello answered. "Our little home is very pleasant, and we have dear and kind friends here -

but I see that we must go."

"Have you decided where to go to?"

"No. That is one of the things I want you to decide for me."

"You cannot bear to live in a large town?"

"Better now probably than I did years ago," Mrs. Costello said, with a faint smile. "I am more used now to a civilized life than I was then."

"I think your best security now, as then, would be found in a crowd - or if you dislike that, you might travel from place to place for a time."

"Are you strong enough for that, mamma?" asked Lucia. "If you are, it is surely the best plan."

"It is the best plan," Mrs. Costello answered, "because it would be a sufficient reason for our leaving here. Only it is a strange time of year to start on such a journey. We must go south, and my not being very strong will be an additional excuse."

"Perhaps," said Mr. Strafford, "your absence need not be a long one. It is quite probable, even now, that Christian may leave the neighbourhood again."

"Why do you say, 'even now?'"

"Because he is so much changed that he appears almost incapable of making many more long journeys."

"You have seen him?"

"I saw him twice. Once he came to my house. You are not afraid to hear all I know?"

"No, no. Pray go on."

"A week or two after I first heard from Mary Wanita of his having appeared on the island, he came one night to my house. As it happened, we met at the door, and I was obliged to let him in. I saw, at once, that he was frightfully changed even from what you remember him. I should have said there was no danger at all to be feared from his attempts to trace you, if I had not perceived that it had become a kind of mania with him, and that his senses, which seem to be completely dulled on other subjects, are still alive on that. He asked me many questions; and although I told him plainly that I would answer none whatever which concerned you, he persisted for a long time, and declared that he knew both you and Lucia were living, and in Canada, and that he meant to find you, and make you come back to the island. With that he went away, and came to me no more; but I saw him one day that I was on this side of the river, sitting in a tavern with some men who looked like lumberers. I asked who they were, and heard that they were a gang in the employ of a man who lives near Cacouna."

Mrs. Costello drew a long breath,

"Could he belong to the gang? In that case he might be near here at any moment."

"He did not then belong to them; but there were two or three other Indians with them, and it struck me that, knowing the river and all the creeks and small streams so well as he does, they would be not unlikely to employ him. I could do nothing further then, however; and other affairs have prevented me from tracing him since."

Lucia had been listening with painful intenseness; Mr. Strafford's fears confirmed her own.

"There are four Indians employed now about the Mills at the other end of the town," she said. "Two of them, I think, are quite young; the third I have hardly seen, but the fourth - " she stopped and then went on steadily, "the fourth looks an old man. He is a wretched object, drunken and half idiotic."

Mr. Strafford looked at her in wonder and trouble. How could he say to a daughter, "You have described your father?" But he felt sure she had done so; and he saw that she guessed it also.

Mrs. Costello had covered her face with her hands; and there was a minute's silence. She was the first to break it.

"We must go at once then," she said. "But how to get away from here without a little delay I do not know."

They wondered that she should speak so, knowing how great her terror of discovery was; but she was thinking of Maurice, and of their last conversation, of his father left in her charge, and of his grief and perplexity if they should go away out of his knowledge, while he was absent, and trusting to them.

Mr. Strafford saw, though he did not understand her hesitation.

"It may be worth while," he said, "for me to run the risk of being seen, and go to-morrow to the employer of these men. Nobody thinks of questioning my right to make any inquires I please about Indians, so that I can easily find out the truth, if you are willing to face the possibility of my meeting Christian, and drawing his attention to you."

Mrs. Costello thought for a moment.

"I thank you," she said. "I wish very much for a little delay if possible. At the worst, if you do meet him, it will be only hasty flight. Can you be prepared for that, Lucia?"

"In an hour, mamma, if necessary. I only wish now to be far away from here."

Her mother's look rested on her sadly. "I do but ask for the delay of a week or two," she said.

But next day, when Mr. Strafford made his inquiry, he brought back news that three or four weeks' delay might be perfectly safe. Christian was, indeed, in the lumberer's employ, but the gang to which he was attached had started for the woods, and would not return for a month. By that time it would be easy to leave the Cottage without hurry, and without attracting unnecessary attention.

CHAPTER XII

"Going away? Nonsense, Elise; you are joking. The very idea of Mrs. Costello going away from Cacouna!"

"She *is* going at any rate, to my sorrow, she and Lucia both; for six months at least, they say."

Mrs. Bellairs and her sister were together again, and Bella, though she was getting used to be called Mrs. Morton, and to see the wedding-ring on her finger, was not at all sobered yet by her matronly state, but might have passed perfectly well for Bella Latour. She and her husband, who had no leisure for a long wedding-tour, had come back to Cacouna the evening before, and were dining to-day at her brother-in-law's. The two ladies were sitting in Mrs. Bellairs' room, and Bella was beginning to hear what little news there was in Cacouna since she went away.

"Where are they going?" she asked when she had had time to believe this surprising item regarding the Costellos.

"South, I believe, for the winter. Mrs. Costello is not well."

"Mrs. Costello or Lucia? Upon my word, if Lucia is not breaking her heart, she ought to be, for Mr. Percy."

"Bella, I wish you would leave off talking such nonsense. Do you never mean to be wiser?"

"Never, my dear; it's hopeless. But confess, Elise, that you were very fidgety about Lucia, and heartily glad to get rid of your visitor. Why, I saw it in every line of your letter, which told me he was gone."

Mrs. Bellairs coloured. "Yes, I will confess I was not sorry when he went; he bored me a little, and I am afraid I was not as hospitable as I might have been."

"Well, and how about Lucia? You might as well tell me, for I shall see her to-morrow and find out everything."

"There is nothing for me to tell or you to find out. Lucia is anxious about her mother, and, I think, sorry to leave Cacouna. There is something like a shadow of real trouble upon her face, and I advise you, Bella, if you have any regard for her, to talk no nonsense to her about Mr. Percy."

Bella looked positively grave for a moment. She was but just married, and was very happy herself - it was natural, perhaps, that she should refuse in her own heart to acknowledge the necessity for Lucia's "real trouble" having other cause than the departure of Percy; but, like her sister, she was very warm-hearted, though her flightiness often concealed it, and she had a small fund of sentiment and romance safely hidden away somewhere, which helped to make her sympathetic.

Mrs. Bellairs was pleased with her sister's gravity. She did not choose to confess that she also believed Lucia had to some degree grieved over her absent admirer, for she knew nothing of his proposal or what had followed it, and had a peculiar dislike to hearing Lucia's name linked with his in Bella's careless talk. But she had seen clearly enough that if he was regretted, that regret was but part of Lucia's trouble, and she wanted to say nothing of her own suspicions, and yet to save Lucia from the attack Bella was sure to make upon her, if she did not perceive (as she was not likely to do unaided) that her jests were specially ill-timed. So she went on talking.

"They are to shut up the Cottage, and I have promised to look into it occasionally and see that it is kept in repair, but I think their greatest difficulty is about poor Mr. Leigh, whom Maurice left in their care. I do not know what he will do without them."

"I suppose there is news of Maurice? You have not sent me any."

"He found his grandfather ill, and in great want of some one of his own family about him; but not, I fancy, at all likely to die. He is slightly paralysed and unable to move without help, or to amuse himself in any way. Poor Maurice seems to have no easy life as far as I can judge."

"Did his grandfather receive him kindly?"

"Very much so, he says. Maurice is like his mother, and that pleased the old man greatly. He introduced him to everybody as his heir."

"Instead of saying 'Poor Maurice,' you ought to say 'Lucky Maurice.' His head will be quite turned."

Mrs. Bellairs smiled. "No fear," she answered. "His heart is in Canada still, and that will keep his head steady."

"What does he say to this move of the Costellos?"

"How can he say anything? It is not three weeks since your marriage, and they knew nothing of it themselves then."

"True, I forgot. I feel as if I had been married a year."

"Not complimentary to the Doctor, if his company is what has made the time seem so long."

"You know very well I don't mean that - only I feel quite settled down into a married woman."

"Do you really? No one would guess it. But what can our two husbands be doing all this time?"

"Here they come. Positively stopping in the hall for a few last words. Treason, no doubt, or they would come in at once, and let us hear."

Treason it was in one sense certainly, for the two gentlemen were discussing a subject which they knew would be displeasing to Bella, if not to both their wives, and which they meant to keep carefully to themselves. It related to Bella's unprofitable farm on Beaver Creek, which her husband was resolved to turn to better account, and from which he had, immediately after his marriage, desired Mr. Bellairs to use the shortest method of ejecting the tenants who now occupied it. Something had already been done, but Doctor Morton fancied too tardily, and he had been urging upon his brother-in-law more vigorous measures. The conclusion of their conversation was this: -

"And I wish, if possible, you would let Clarkson understand that it is quite useless to send his wife to plague Bella. She agrees with me that women had better always leave business to their husbands, and I have no intention of letting her be humbugged out of her property."

"Very well," said Mr. Bellairs, not altogether pleased with this speech, "only I warn you, Clarkson is an awkward fellow to deal with, and if you do turn him out, you may expect him to revenge himself in any and every way he can."

Doctor Morton laughed. "I give him leave," he said. "As long as Bella knows nothing of the matter, it will not trouble me."

With that he opened the door, and came into the room where his bride sat entirely unsuspicious of his intentions, or of the way in which her own innocent words had been made use of.

What Magdalen Scott had said of Doctor Morton on his

wedding-day was perfectly true - he was a hard man. Not cruel or unjust, but keen and hard. He did no wrong to any one. He could even be liberal and considerate in his dealings with those who could not wrong him; but he had neither forbearance nor mercy for those who defrauded him in any way whatever of his rights. He was fond of his wife, being his wife, but if she had been poor he would never have thought of marrying her. Her possessions were, plainly and honestly, of as much value to him as herself. He would tolerate the loss of the one as soon as that of the other. The farm at Beaver Creek was the only thing she had brought him which was not in a satisfactory state; it had cost him considerable thought during their short engagement, and being extremely prompt and business-like in his ideas, he had made up his mind that the land should be cleared at once of intruders, that the wood might be cut down during the winter, and cultivation begin with the following spring. Having decided upon this, he was not a person to be turned from his plan by difficulties. He thought both Mr. Latour and Mr. Bellairs had been remiss in their work of dealing with the squatters, and felt a sort of resentment against them for having taken such negligent care of *his* property. He did not like at present to go so far as to take the case entirely out of his brother-in-law's hands, but he had decided that it would be necessary himself to look after, and urge on, the proceedings which were being taken against Clarkson.

He determined, therefore, that the first time he could spare an hour or two from his profession, he would ride over alone to Beaver Creek, and see precisely the condition of the land, and what inroads had been made upon it by Clarkson and the Indians. It was only a day or two later that he carried out his intention; and after a few early visits to patients, turned his horse's head along the road which, following the general direction of the river bank, led towards Beaver Creek. He rode tolerably fast for two or three miles, and then began to slacken his pace, and look round him with greater interest. He was still some distance from the creek itself, but the land lay on this side of it, and he was curious to know the condition of the neighbouring farms. He had not been very long resident in

Cacouna, and was but little acquainted with the country in this direction, except where, here and there, he had paid professional visits.

But at last he arrived at what he knew by description must be his wife's property, and his examination began in good earnest. For the most part, however, there was nothing to examine except timber, and that of little value. "Plenty of firewood," was his only comment as he went on. Beyond the belt of wood, however, he came upon a clear space bordering the creek, and strewed with decayed fish, fragments of old nets, and broken pieces of wood - traces of the use to which the Indians were in the habit of putting it. A small hut stood just in the shelter of the bush, but it was empty, and the whole place had the look of being not inhabited, but only visited occasionally for fishing.

A rough cart-track led past the hut and towards the mouth of the creek. Along this Doctor Morton turned, and soon came in sight of the log-house which Clarkson had built upon the very best corner of the land. It was by no means an uncomfortable-looking dwelling. The rough logs were partly covered by a wild vine, and a quantity of hop plants, still green and leafy. The roof, instead of shingles, was thatched with sheets of bark, and an iron stove pipe passing through these was the only visible chimney. But the place had a well-to-do look, which was not likely to improve the Doctor's good humour. There was a little garden roughly railed in, in front, and some children playing there. At the end of the house was a small farm-yard, with pigs, a cow, and a shaggy horse, all looking out serenely at the stranger. Each one of the occupants of the place seemed to feel perfectly secure and at home, and to have neither suspicion nor fear of the speedy ejection which was being planned for them. No doubt it was very absurd, but even the serene sleepy eyes of the cow seemed to have aggravation in them, and the Doctor turned his horse round to return home, in the worst possible humour.

The country roads were so bad, however, that though it always appears natural for a man in a passion to ride fast, he was obliged to check his horse and pick his way among the deep ruts and holes. Going on in this way and having some little trouble with the animal, which was young and spirited, he saw a man coming along the road before him, and as they drew nearer recognized Clarkson.

The squatter was not a pleasant man to look at. He was of middle height, very broadly and strongly built, but with a slouching gait which corresponded perfectly with the expression of his coarse features, half brutal, half sly. He wore an old fur cap, drawn so low upon his forehead as to shade his eyes, and conceal the frown with which he perceived his enemy. His usual audacity of manner, however, did not desert him. He stood still as the other approached, and called out,

"Good morning, Doctor. Been looking at your property?"

"Yes," was the answer. "And I have one thing to say to you, the sooner you are off it the better."

"Now, that ain't reasonable," Clarkson said, coming nearer. "I've built a bit of a house there, and took a world of trouble, and you expect me to give it up for nothing."

"Decidedly I do. Good morning."

He was moving on, when Clarkson caught his rein.

"Look here, Doctor Morton," he said, "I found the land wild as land could be. I took possession of it, and kept it. Mr. Latour was not hard upon me, nor Miss Latour neither; and I can't see why you as has had nothing to do with it, neither buying it, nor building on it, should be so much keener after it than them."

"I don't mean to argue the matter," the Doctor answered. "You've had warning enough; and I mean you to go. Loose my horse."

Clarkson's face was growing darker every moment. He held the bridle more firmly, and began to speak again.

Doctor Morton suddenly raised his riding-whip, and let the handle fall sharply on the hand that detained him; at the same moment he spurred his horse, and the animal, springing forward, struck Clarkson with its shoulder and sent him staggering back across the road. He recovered himself in a moment, and darted forward with an oath, but it was too late - horse and rider were already far beyond his reach.

Doctor Morton went straight to Mr. Bellairs' office. He felt it needful to get rid, in some way, of his new irritation against Clarkson, but some consciousness of being for the moment urged on by personal dislike, made him say nothing of their encounter. He merely satisfied himself that his brother-in-law, considerably piqued by the implied blame which had been thrown upon his guardianship, was now doing all that was possible to satisfy his eagerness.

After all these affairs it was late when he reached home. He and Bella were going to dine out, and she was waiting impatiently for him when he finished his day's work and went in to dress. He had no time to talk to her then, and kept what he had to say for their drive; but as they drove along, it occurred to him that if he told her of his meeting with Clarkson she would worry herself, and perhaps him also, so he finally kept it to himself altogether, and as his ill-humour subsided it passed out of his mind.

Choose from Thousands of 1stWorldLibrary Classics By

A. M. Barnard
Ada Leverson
Adolphus William Ward
Aesop
Agatha Christie
Alexander Aaronsohn
Alexander Kielland
Alexandre Dumas
Alfred Gatty
Alfred Ollivant
Alice Duer Miller
Alice Turner Curtis
Alice Dunbar
Ambrose Bierce
Amelia E. Barr
Amory H. Bradford
Andrew Lang
Andrew McFarland Davis
Andy Adams
Anna Sewell
Annie Besant
Annie Hamilton Donnell
Annie Payson Call
Annonaymous
Anton Chekhov
Arnold Bennett
Arthur Conan Doyle
Arthur M. Winfield
Arthur Ransome
Atticus
B.H. Baden-Powell
B. M. Bower
Baroness Emmuska Orczy
Baroness Orczy
Basil King
Bayard Taylor
Ben Macomber
Bertha Muzzy Bower
Bjornstjerne Bjornson
Booth Tarkington
Boyd Cable
Bram Stoker
C. Collodi
C. E. Orr
C. M. Ingleby
Carolyn Wells
Catherine Parr Traill
Charles A. Eastman
Charles Dickens

Charles Dudley Warner
Charles Farrar Browne
Charles Ives
Charles Kingsley
Charles Klein
Charles Amory Beach
Charles Hanson Towne
Charles Lathrop Pack
Charles Whibley
Charles Willing Beale
Charlotte M. Braeme
Charlotte M. Yonge
Charlotte Perkins Stetson
Clair W. Hayes
Clarence Day Jr.
Clarence E. Mulford
Clemence Housman
Confucius
Cornelis DeWitt Wilcox
Cyril Burleigh
D. H. Lawrence
Daniel Defoe
David Garnett
Dinah Craik
Don Carlos Janes
Donald Keyhoe
Dorothy Kilner
Dougan Clark
Douglas Fairbanks
E. Nesbit
E.P.Roe
E. Phillips Oppenheim
Earl Barnes
Edgar Rice Burroughs
Edith Van Dyne
Edith Wharton
Edward J. O'Biren
Edward S. Ellis
Edwin L. Arnold
Eleanor Atkins
Eliot Gregory
Elizabeth Gaskell
Elizabeth McCracken
Elizabeth Von Arnim
Ellem Key
Emerson Hough
Emilie F. Carlen
Emily Dickinson
Enid Bagnold

Enilor Macartney Lane
Erasmus W. Jones
Ernie Howard Pie
Ethel Turner
Ethel Watts Mumford
Eugenie Foa
Eugene Wood
Eustace Hale Ball
Evelyn Everett-green
Everard Cotes
F. H. Cheley
F. J. Cross
Federick Austin Ogg
Ferdinand Ossendowski
Francis Bacon
Francis Darwin
Frances Hodgson Burnett
Frances Parkinson Keyes
Frank Gee Patchin
Frank Harris
Frank Jewett Mather
Frank L. Packard
Frank V. Webster
Frederic Stewart Isham
Frederick Trevor Hill
Frederick Winslow Taylor
Friedrich Kerst
Friedrich Nietzsche
Fyodor Dostoyevsky
G.A. Henty
G.K. Chesterton
Gabrielle E. Jackson
Garrett P. Serviss
Gaston Leroux
George A. Warren
George Ade
Geroge Bernard Shaw
George Durston
George Ebers
George Eliot
George Gissing
George MacDonald
George Meredith
George Orwell
George Sylvester Viereck
George Tucker
George W. Cable
George Wharton James
Gertrude Atherton

Grace E. King
Grace Gallatin
Grant Allen
Guillermo A. Sherwell
Gulielma Zollinger
Gustav Flaubert
H. A. Cody
H. B. Irving
H.C. Bailey
H. G. Wells
H. H. Munro
H. Irving Hancock
H. Rider Haggard
H. W. C. Davis
Hamilton Wright Mabie
Hans Christian Andersen
Harold Avery
Harold McGrath
Harriet Beecher Stowe
Harry Houidini
Helent Hunt Jackson
Helen Nicolay
Hendrik Conscience
Hendy David Thoreau
Henri Barbusse
Henrik Ibsen
Henry Adams
Henry Ford
Henry Frost
Henry James
Henry Jones Ford
Henry Seton Merriman
Henry W Longfellow
Herbert A. Giles
Herbert N. Casson
Herman Hesse
Homer
Honore De Balzac
Horace Walpole
Horatio Alger Jr.
Howard Pyle
Howard R. Garis
Hugh Lofting
Hugh Walpole
Humphry Ward
Ian Maclaren
Inez Haynes Gillmore
Irving Bacheller
Israel Abrahams
Ivan Turgenev
J.G.Austin

J. Henri Fabre
J. M. Barrie
J. Macdonald Oxley
J. S. Fletcher
J. S. Knowles
J. Storer Clouston
Jack London
Jacob Abbott
James Allen
James Andrews
James Baldwin
James DeMille
James Joyce
James Lane Allen
James Lane Allen
James Oliver Curwood
James Oppenheim
James Otis
James R. Driscoll
Jane Austen
Janet Aldridge
Jens Peter Jacobsen
Jerome K. Jerome
John Burroughs
John Cournos
John F. Kennedy
John Gay
John Glasworthy
John Habberton
John Joy Bell
John Kendrick Bangs
John Milton
John Philip Sousa
Jonas Lauritz Idemil Lie
Jonathan Swift
Joseph A. Altsheler
Joseph Carey
Joseph Conrad
Joseph E. Badger Jr
Joseph Hergesheimer
Joseph Jacobs
Jules Vernes
Julian Hawthrone
Julie A Lippmann
Justin Huntly McCarthy
Kakuzo Okakura
Kenneth Grahame
Kenneth McGaffey
Kate Langley Bosher
Kate Langley Bosher
Katherine Cecil Thurston

Katherine Stokes
L. A. Abbot
L. T. Meade
L. Frank Baum
Latta Griswold
Laura Lee Hope
Laurence Housman
Lawrence Beasley
Leo Tolstoy
Leonid Andreyev
Lewis Carroll
Lewis Sperry Chafer
Lilian Bell
Lloyd Osbourne
Louis Hughes
Louis Tracy
Louisa May Alcott
Lucy Fitch Perkins
Lucy Maud Montgomery
Lydia Miller Middleton
Lyndon Orr
M. Corvus
M. H. Adams
Margaret E. Sangster
Margaret Vandercook
Margret Penrose
Maria Edgeworth
Maria Thompson Daviess
Mariano Azuela
Marion Polk Angellotti
Mark Overton
Mark Twain
Mary Austin
Mary Catherine Crowley
Mary Cole
Mary Hastings Bradley
Mary Roberts Rinehart
Mary Rowlandson
M. Wollstonecraft Shelley
Maud Lindsay
Max Beerbohm
Myra Kelly
Nathaniel Hawthrone
Nicolo Machiavelli
O. F. Walton
Oscar Wilde
Owen Johnson
P.G. Wodehouse
Paul and Mabel Thorne
Paul G. Tomlinson
Paul Severing

Percy Brebner
Peter B. Kyne
Plato
R. Derby Holmes
R. L. Stevenson
R. S. Ball
Rabindranath Tagore
Rahul Alvares
Ralph Bonehill
Ralph Henry Barbour
Ralph Victor
Ralph Waldo Emmerson
Rene Descartes
Rex Beach
Rex E. Beach
Richard Harding Davis
Richard Jefferies
Richard Le Gallienne
Robert Barr
Robert Frost
Robert Gordon Anderson
Robert L. Drake
Robert Lansing
Robert Lynd
Robert Michael Ballantyne
Robert W. Chambers
Rosa Nouchette Carey
Rudyard Kipling
Samuel B. Allison

Samuel Hopkins Adams
Sarah Bernhardt
Sarah C. Hallowell
Selma Lagerlof
Sherwood Anderson
Sigmund Freud
Standish O'Grady
Stanley Weyman
Stella Benson
Stephen Crane
Stewart Edward White
Stijn Streuvels
Swami Abhedananda
Swami Parmananda
T. S. Ackland
T. S. Arthur
The Princess Der Ling
Thomas A. Janvier
Thomas A Kempis
Thomas Anderton
Thomas Bailey Aldrich
Thomas Bulfinch
Thomas De Quincey
Thomas H. Huxley
Thomas Hardy
Thomas More
Thornton W. Burgess
U. S. Grant
Valentine Williams

Various Authors
Vaughan Kester
Victor Appleton
Virginia Woolf
Walter Camp
Walter Scott
Washington Irving
Wilbur Lawton
Wilkie Collins
Willa Cather
Willard F. Baker
William Dean Howells
William le Queux
W. Makepeace Thackeray
William W. Walter
Winston Churchill
Yei Theodora Ozaki
Yogi Ramacharaka
Young E. Allison
Zane Grey

www.ingramcontent.com/pod-product-compliance
Lightning Source LLC
Chambersburg PA
CBHW031349170626
46807CB00002B/884